THE
GILL
NETTERS

BY
JOLIE PAYLIN

Jacket Illustration by
ANNE NOLAN

HILLSDALE EDUCATIONAL PUBLISHERS
HILLSDALE, MICHIGAN
1979

Jolie Paylin is also the author of *Cutover Country* and *Nels Oskar*.

Jacket illustration by Anne Nolan
Lansing, Michigan

First edition, 1979

Library of Congress Cataloging in Publication Data

Paylin, Jolie, 1913-
      The Gill Netters.
      I. Title
813 ′ .5 ′4   79-89031
ISBN   0-910726-82-5

1. Commercial fishing—Fiction
2. Michigan & Wisconsin—Fiction

Contents

1

On Ice and Driven Sea

"Who told you those women followed Aaron home from the war?" Leander Johannsen stood in the canvas lifting shanty and watched his uncle pull a gill net from a hole chiseled in the ice of Green Bay.

Stephan Eckberg picked a six-pound whitefish from the meshes and threw it flopping into a wooden box. "Everybody in Ephraim knows your boy brought a young woman, her little girl and an old black woman home from the blue-gray war."

Leander ran a bare finger up one of the crevasses dividing his windburned face into an expressive puzzle and pushed a knitted chook back on his roan hair. "Stephan, that is no way to fool a person."

"I'm not fooling. I only want you to tell Helga before some neighbor brings her the news."

"Where do you think Aaron keeps so many women?"

"In Menominee. The young woman works in the Quimby House."

Bending over, the older man passed the long curtain of net, cedar floats and lead sinkers between his leather hip boots. The silver-scaled fish came out of the bay with such satisfying regularity that he'd forgotten about the cold water on his arthritic hands.

Leander sat on a ledge above a runner of their mobile tent, the wind taken from his sails. "I knew it!" he cried. "There had to be a reason for Aaron going to that sawmill town. He could've learned coopering in Fish Creek, an easy walk from home."

"A man goes where his woman is," Stephan reminded him.

"And I worried all winter for fear it was my fault Aaron left home."

1

As his sons had grown older, Leander had tried to quell his strong tendency to dominate so the boys could learn self sufficiency. He'd been especially careful with Aaron—a hard war had taught his second son to think for himself. He'd seen his brother Henning die in that conflict.

Sitting there, observing Stephan, his mind went back. Ten years before, in the middle '50's, they'd emigrated from the Island of Fano off the Jutland Peninsula of Denmark to a virgin timbered inlet on the western shore of the Door Peninsula of Wisconsin. Except for a claustrophobic ride in the hold of a clipper ship, the journey for their family of eight had been uneventful.

Now the Johannsen fishery was thriving for there was no end to the lake trout, whitefish and herring. But he'd begun to feel the toil of his nearly sixty years after his second and third sons had gone off to enlist in the army in Madison. Until the past fall, the war had been the only knot in his unwinding skein of plans.

Olaf, his firstborn, should have been the cooper they needed to provide a reliable supply of salt fish kegs. He had a leg shortened by a boyhood injury and more patience with woodworking. But Aaron had stood his ground. The reason was now clear—but a black woman and a child too?

"Well, Stephan, I'll tell you something." He jumped up and helped himself to a serving of their catch browning on a tiny sheet-iron stove. "Our Aaron lad has some explaining to do. This crew'll just have to lift nets with one horse and the sail sled tomorrow. I'll take the mare and jumper and go over the ice to the Michigan side of the bay and see what he has to say."

Passing the shanty horse dozing in the February sun, Leander left Stephan and walked eighty paces to the next lifting hole with his ice chisel and shovel. The hundred-mile-long bay resembled a snow-covered tundra thinly studded with small evergreen tree net markers. Distant specks moving like peregrinating badgers were oxen, men and horses working around snow camouflaged fishing shanties.

Olaf and Bjorn's claybank gelding was hauling their shanty to the rendevous at the bobsleigh parked northwest of tadpole-shaped Chambers Island.

Turning away, shielding his eyes from the brilliant rays reflected from the snow, he looked to the somber wilderness shore of Michigan. He could make out the old Indian clearing where he planned to build a new fishery as soon as the frost was out of the ground. But first Aaron had to learn to make barrels out of the white pine and black ash standing behind the roadless beachhead.

He planned? What if Aaron could not master the difficult craft of coopering? Many men could not. What was he getting his family into? Well, it was not his fault the whitefish had migrated.

He shook himself and ceased his woolgathering. Anxious to start the long haul back to Helga, he resumed his work with energy. His Finlander-Swede wife, a pretty, capable and pleasant grandmother with soft-piled dark hair and intensely blue eyes, had been ailing since October. Using the long-handled chisel, he chipped at the new ice in the hole beneath a forked crutch holding up the ends of the last two nets of his and Stephan's gang.

Walking behind the now double-hitched horses heading back to Ephraim with the loaded sleigh, Leander thought of Helga. He remembered her running over the bumpy ground between her garden and the squat peeled-cedar log house hunkered on a rise above an unnamed indentation on the shoreline separating Fish Creek and Ephraim. She'd just washed her knee length hair and had been drying it in the sun. The unbraided tresses had drifted like a banner and her small white terrier had leaped with joy beside her.

Helga and their daughter Anna had never been homesick as Stephan and the boys had been. The two women had always looked for new birds, plants and trees, and Stephan had devised a wind driven tumbler to polish the pretty stones they found in the cove. Before Annie had married a farmer near Green Bay, she'd helped her mother grub a space for flowers and fruit trees bought from an itinerant nurseryman. Lilac bushes at the front corners of the house had bloomed for the first time the past spring.

As they approached their home pier on the Wisconsin promontory, diverse rigs fanned out to the long fishing settlement. It was good to see wood smoke swirling from both the cooking and heating chimneys on the building that was more of a hut than a house but was made supremely habitable by their wife and mother.

He'd dreamed of erecting a high white house for Helga above the bluff in Stephan's cow pasture, but now fate had stepped in. However, the new invention, a sewing machine she'd mentioned so often, should be hers—and the reed organ she secretly coveted. He'd not come home from his errand tomorrow without them.

Helga was having one of her brief spells of well-being. She'd have the cow milked and a good supper ready for the table. The hungry boys would make short work of unloading the fish, the sooner to get at the food.

Parting from Stephan where the shoveled-snow path branched to the older man's coop of pigs and chickens, Leander put the team in the shed with the cow. If he hurried with the unharnessing and feeding, he could have a few minutes alone with Helga in the large communal room that was the heart of their home.

Helga turned from the pine work cupboard with a smile and a little welcoming gesture of her hand. "Good, you're here ahead of the rest. I need to talk to you."

Wearing a billowing, starched blue calico dress topped with a white apron, she came quickly to the table with a cup of hot coffee and a wild butternut pastry to stave off his hunger till suppertime.

He dropped into one of the pine chairs Stephan had carved and doweled and removed his thigh-high boots as the rest must do to prevent extra work with the scraped plank floor and the colorful braided rugs. As he set his footwear by the great limestone fireplace, a consuming anger at the headlong rush of time overtook him and he turned to hold his wife in his arms with an ardor that showed no signs of abating after more than a quarter century of marriage.

Helga knew about Aaron! But he must be casual. "Well, tell me," he said. "Is your news good or bad?"

"Good for me at least," she replied. "Do you think we could borrow the Olsons' cutter and go to the stores in Marinette and Menominee tomorrow if the weather's as nice as it has been today? Maybe we could have dinner at the Quimby House."

He released her to savor the freshly roasted and ground coffee. "Who told you about Aaron?"

"I've known since he came home to visit with us two weeks ago. He told me himself, but he wanted to see how things turned out before he talked to you."

"He thinks I'm such a bad papa, I don't understand."

"I wanted him to tell you all he told me about the women he brought from Tennessee. I said you'd like Liza, little Naomi and Garnet who is a mulatto woman. It's not us. He's afraid they're lonesome for their southern homeland. He plans to marry Liza right away in the spring if they stay through the winter cold and snow. He'll have to bring them to Ephraim while the ice is still safe for travel."

"How do you think those women got way up here? The little girl belongs to him?"

"Liza's husband died from the war. Aaron met her when he stole her cow for army beef. Naomi was more than a year old at the time."

"My boy would never steal!"

"That war was too bad to talk about. When Aaron was discharged, he went back to find Liza and see Henning's grave in a Baptist churchyard nearby before he came home to us. He gave her money and wrote to her when he found a cottage for her in Menominee. He was able to find her a job at the hotel not far from Herr Braun's cooperage where he learns to make barrels. She wouldn't come unless she could support herself."

"What do you suppose she looks like? I bet she don't have red hair."

"Aaron says Liza's people have lived in the back hills of Tennessee and Virginia for a hundred and fifty years, but she carries herself like a queen's lady. She's tall and slim with black hair and gray eyes and she favors her grandfather who was an Indian from the Smoky Mountains region. Naomi is four and looks just like her."

"But Aaron is not tall, and worse yet, he'll look like me someday."

"You should know by now that love doesn't go where it's sent."

"Do you think we'll get along with her?"

"Her ways are strange. Aaron says she speaks the most confusing form of English he's ever heard. She sounds like the English mackerelmen who were shipwrecked off Fano."

"Well, Henning died for the black woman, and we need a child around here. This Liza, I bet she talks no worse than me and Stephan. You're right. We'll go to Menominee in the morning but we'll stay overnight. The trip would be too much for you in one day. Besides, it'll take some time for you to pick out a sewing machine and an organ."

"Leander!" Helga glowed with joy. "You don't mean it!"

Leander sat in front of a wide window facing the bay, smoothing the polished wood of a trestle table Stephan had sawed, planed and trunneled from a single white pine bole. "The boys are coming," he announced. Like them, he was starved. The aroma of Helga's spicy pork and potato sausage made his stomach jump.

Stephan bowed his gray head when everyone had been seated. Leander glanced at Bjorn who at fifteen was going to be the red-headed Viking of the family. God would forgive Stephan if he only said, "We thank you, Lord," as he sometimes did. No boy could work so hard and grow so fast without being famished.

For the thousandth time, Leander felt a twinge of guilt as he picked up his fork—he'd not even once returned thanks for the food since Stephan came with them in America.

Now the days were lengthening and the men would go back to the fish house after supper to gut and salt their catch. When they came again to Helga's fireside, she'd welcome them with the golden light of her new coal oil lamps.

That doctor in Green Bay was out of his mind. Helga would always be where her lamps were; and those lights would be seen across the bay on the Michigan shore where the Johannsen clan would prosper in health and substance. No, that was a lie. An invisible invader had made it so.

His lower lip began to quiver; he pinched it between his thumb and forefinger and went to the cupboard where he rummaged for a crock of jam. Forty years, he'd lived a man's life of calculated risks and done a man's work on fragile pavements of ice and wind-driven seas, and now calamity and a shoal of women would knock his whole world galley-west.

2

And Still Be in Bed

This April morning, spring had come to the cove near Ephraim. At the breakfast table, Helga Johannsen said to her guests from Tennessee, "Ladies, this is the day our men come home from their new landing. With no contrary winds, the voyage'll only take a few hours."

Four days earlier, the Johannsen men had departed in two sail work boats to Aaron's property on the Michigan shore to cut building logs for cabins they hoped would be ready for occupancy by the first of June. The women had taken on Stephan's and Bjorn's chores and after the meal they went out to the barns together. Helga's terrier Tippy streaked in ecstatic circles around Naomi, yipping enticements for her to play with him.

Liza Peake watched her little girl run ahead with the dog then dart back to talk with Aaron's mother. In the five weeks of their stay with the Johannsens, Naomi had become attached to her new "Grandma", and Helga had reciprocated with enchanting stories and games.

Walking along the snow-freed path, looking across to a bluff where rising sap had caused the topmost twigs of birch and soft maple to be tinged with rose, Liza knew she'd never met so gay and gentle a person. Only then did she remember Aaron had said his mother had gone to a doctor in Green Bay in the fall. She stole a look at Helga's merry eyes and decided they were the color of the indigo Garnet had used to dye the woof threads of a handwoven shawl she'd kept hidden from motley marauders during the war. If Aaron's mother became really ill, as he feared she might, they could help her. Garnet had a poke of herbs and medicinals and there was healing in her coffee-brown hands.

Almost without warning to the women in the house, at eleven o'clock the sun dimmed and a stiff northeast wind churned the bay and flung hail at the window panes. Liza got up from the new sewing machine where she'd been running long petticoat seams and went to the window. Turning, striving to keep any silly apprehension from her tone, she spoke, "Mrs. Johannsen, do you reckon the men'll take their boats out on that water efen hit keeps blowen like that?"

"Don't worry," Aaron's mother replied in calm reassurance from the table where she stitched by hand on Liza's thin, sky-blue wool wedding dress. "Stephan can smell a storm for hours before it strikes. They're either safe at Aaron's creek or they'll be ashore here any minute."

As Liza sat again at the machine, she heard Garnet grumble to Naomi. They both stood at a counter under a north window where Garnet was kneading bread for the men's larder. Naomi was wadding a child's loaf and chattering about the pretty snow that had just blossomed from the hail.

The short, sinewy woman hated snow. "Hain't no man wuth all dis winter-in-summer and de trouble pounden riz bread," she complained.

"Now Garnet," Liza chided, "you know Aaron's Uncle Stephan prizes light bread more than purty women."

Helga had risen from the table and was staring out the window as the gathering storm snowed and rained by turns. Then, while she was standing there, the precipitation ceased and the cold sun laid an ominous halo around the tops of the hemlocks hugging the cliff south of the house. When she left the window, she said, "You know, I'd like to walk along the beach and up the cowpath to my favorite spot in the cedar woods on the bluff shoulder. Some exercise and fresh air would do me good."

"You be worryen, hain't you?" Liza asked. "You can see the whole lake from up there?"

"I didn't mean to upset you, Liza," Aaron's mother continued matter-of-factly. "I have no true reason to be fearful. By now I should know that wherever it pleases God to make earth basins and fill them with water, there'll be perverse winds and storms and men who feel obliged to make their living on them. Some men can take water or leave it, but the Johannsen men will work on it and die on it or as close as they can get and still be in bed."

Helga went on, "I think the wind's subsiding. Would any of

you like to come up on the bluff with me? I can smell arbutus. A bouquet in a toothpick holder would perfume this house. But we'll have to bundle up—in spite of the sun, it'll be damp and chilly outside.

Garnet was holding back from joining the outing. Liza knew it was still hard for her dark companion to believe she was accepted as an equal in her new home.

"You too, Garnet," Helga encouraged warmly.

Dressed in the wraps they'd worn in winter, they all left the house and moved across the sleet-dusted dry grass of the yard to the fish house where they climbed an ice-capped pole fence. As they hiked through a belt of creeping juniper on the beach, they watched the tumbling clouds and listened to the spring heralding cries of a single killdeer. They turned from the slamming sea and scrambled up the steep, wet cowpath, aiding their progress by catching hold of tough leatherwood bushes.

Clutching encumbering skirts, Liza and Garnet were at home on the rocky terrain but they paced themselves to stay with Helga. Then, seeing their guide gasp for breath, Liza swung herself up and around through birch trunks made opaline by the strangely filtered sun and stepped ahead in the root-bridged track to hold out her hand.

Naomi lagged behind, playing with Tippy who ran furiously between her and Helga, offering sticks to both.

At the top of the bluff, as they leaned against large cedars bordering a stumpy pasture, Liza said, "Mrs. Johannsen, I knowed you weren't truly hankeren for the posies you spoke of." Sweeping her hand skyward, she went on, "Hit be a 'weatheren up there, hain't hit?"

"I'm not really distressed," Helga answered. "I just wanted to look for sails with red stripes."

"I reckon God be up there. We can trust on that."

"I agree with you, Liza, but I think we'd better go back to the house as soon as we find a sprig of arbutus for Naomi. Look, there under that balsam tree, I see a vine peeking out from the dead needles at the edge of that old snowbank."

The sun had capriciously disappeared and pellets of sleet stung their faces. They started down the precipitous path in the worsening storm with Naomi grasping a few pinkish flowerlets and a tendril of green leaves. There were no sails on the water—every prudent sailor on the bay had gone ashore.

3

Quadroon Sailor Boys

Arriving with excitement at Aaron's landing, Leander was briefly disappointed; the brook was no more than a swamp draining rill channeling its way from virgin timber through an old Indian cornfield to the beach. But the day was too fair for fretting, and he concentrated on the shelter that must be built by nightfall.

Bjorn, Olaf and Stephan dropped anchor from the flat bottomed pound boat, the *Silver Guld,* and waded ashore, while he and Aaron poled the cleverly hulled *Liten Flicka* around the bend of the freshet filled stream to a protected mooring. A slip would have to be dredged and shored with hemlock piling before the *Guld* could be tied up properly.

Once ashore, Leander made an exploratory lope around the area north of the small creek, searching for sites for the homes and sheds they must construct for the new fishery. Aaron and Bjorn, Olaf and Stephan had paired off to dig holes and set two massive mooring posts cut from sentinel cedars standing nearby.

When Leander came back, he declared loudly so there would be no misunderstanding, "We'll make both of our houses on this side of the crick by those birches in from the bay. Hemlocks draw lightning," he added, referring to the lofty trees topping an understory of young mixed hardwoods on the south side of the stream.

While Olaf laid a cooking fire, Stephan tied a line from the starboard bow of the *Liten Flicka* to a pillar of cedar, taking his time before he said, "Then I'll put Garnet's and my cabin on the south side and we'll cut the hemlocks." He'd waited till the last possible moment to announce his intention of having a dwelling of his own.

Caught by surprise, Leander demanded of his elderly uncle, "What did you say?" Then he forgot himself. "You'd marry a nigger? You're too old, even for a white woman!"

Stephan was rigid with anger as he retorted, "Who said from marry? We'll live in a house of our own and raise quadroon sailor boys and pretty girls with blue eyes and curly hair. Shame on you, Leander, for saying "nigger". When you look as good as Garnet, I'll let you know."

Leander found himself blustering in retaliation, "I don't think the old sow had any trouble taking care of those two extra runt pigs. I think you wanted to get Garnet away from the rest of us at feeding time."

Stephan pushed the Scandinavian style, short-visored cap back on his sparse graying red hair and answered cooly, "We're not in that much of a hurry. We'll take our time and wait for a roof and feather bed. Garnet has Tennessee goose feathers." He picked up an ax leaning against the mooring post. "I'll help Olaf cut poles for our shack. If we don't want to sleep on the cold ground tonight, we'd better get a crib and rafters ready for a canvas roof and make some bunks."

With that, the oldest member of the crew marched off. Leander was sorry he had talked smart, even if Stephan had said the words initiating the exchange.

Stephan knew about Helga. One day he, Leander, had surprised him at the workbench in the twine shed. The elderly man had tried to unconcernedly pull an old jib sail over a bundle of pine boards painstakingly planed and dovetailed, and stow them under the bench. But Leander had seen the boards were marked to be quickly assembled in a narrow hexagonal box six feet long.

Only God knew who the box was for and when it would be needed. But it would be. As sure as the sun went down beyond the wilderness reaching unbroken to the Dakota prairies, the day would come. You couldn't count on fish, the weather, your fellow men or even yourself. There was only one certainty in this world—life began to end the moment you were born.

Leander knew Stephan favored Olaf who was so much like Helga, though the young man restrained his lively spirits and strove for manly reticence. It was too bad Olaf couldn't've gone off to war and met a girl like Liza. Now, because of a fall in his youth from an apple tree in Denmark, he limped and ignored all women except his mother and sister. His worthy seed had been locked away as effectively as Stephan's had been over nothing at all but a notion for footloose freedom.

Aaron and Bjorn were heading with the axes to a fringe of aspens near the tall forest west of the aboriginal cornfield. As Leander started to dig a twelve-by-fifteen-foot rectangular sill groove in the sod close to the brook, he overheard Stephan speak to Olaf, "Come, you and me, we'll show Aaron and Bjorn how to cut popple." Then the old man stood in his tracks in an attitude of thought. "Well, cut is fine," he remarked, "but who is going to be the skidding horse and drag the poles across that field? Where is our Kate and Buck?"

Leander rammed the shovel blade in the ground with his foot. The clearing was wider and the aspens bigger than he'd remembered, but they had to have a shelter for the night. He should have been sharper in his planning. He was slipping.

"Uncle Stephan," Olaf was speaking to his granduncle's back as they moved off to the woods, "I heard what you said about Garnet. I'll help you build your cottage. You'll need a bridge too if you make your place on the far side of the stream. We'll work on that after suppers."

"Olaf," Stephan asked, and Leander had to strain his ears to hear this bit of conversation, "do you think her black color makes Kate an ugly horse? Well, I am old enough to look under a woman's skin and see what's in her heart."

Leander swore. They had carried, pulled and peavied aspen logs across the five acre meadow for the initial building of their fishery complex. "By God!" he exploded, "I may look like Old Buck, but I will not do his work!"

Aaron sat on the butt end of a twenty-foot log, gathering his strength. "Are you going to tie Buck up like a sack of potatoes and haul him over here in an open pound boat?"

Leander had an answer for that, "Tomorrow the first thing, I'll walk on the beach to Cedar Forks and find that Swanson feller we talked to on the ice last winter. His oxen may not be so good for gill nets, but maybe we can get him to bring the beasts and skid logs."

"What if Swanson has use for his oxen?"

"Then we'll push our plans up. You and Liza can get married and ride the horses around the Green Bay shore like we said we'd have to do when the ice went out so fast."

"No! I'll quit first!" Aaron struck his knees with the palms of his hands and shot to his feet. "I didn't coax Liza to come to this forsaken wilderness to ride a horse a hundred and seventy miles on a cold, wet honeymoon. I said *maybe* we would do it when the weather settled off warm. If we move the horses now, Bjorn'll have to help me."

"All right! I'll find some sort of beast in the morning—I won't come back from the Forks without some power." Swiveling his wrists and ax as indicated, Leander cut a precise notch in the bottom log and rolled it into the shallow trench with his toe. Only a few weeks before, he'd have met Aaron's ultimatum with the tart question, "Who's running this business?" Now age and disaster were forcing him to accede to his sons' ideas. Before long, he would be looking for a hole to curl up in as Stephan and Garnet were now.

4

Unless We Get a Miracle

At daybreak ending their first night in the shack, Aaron Johannsen lay in his rigid bed and waited for his father to return from an early visit to the latrine behind a young hemlock near the *Guld's* mooring post. Stephan had hastily contrived the facility by digging a hole between two birch trees and felling them across it and onto fish boxes at each end. Was his father sick? It was said that was how a heart seizure sometimes came on—having to move one's bowels before the normal time to get up in the morning. No one would dally in a frosty, open air privy that long.

Aaron climbed down from his top bunk fully clothed except for his boots. Outdoors, the air was bracing and full of the fresh feel of spring; it would be a good day for a man to begin work on his first home. He walked along the brook bank to the felled birches. The makeshift outhouse was empty.

On impulse, he strode around a cluster of sapling aspen and through a mat of beach juniper in time to catch sight of his father hiking past some cedars on a bouldery spit of sand. It was no use to call him back. You couldn't run behind Leander Johannsen like a nanny woman—that would be outright questioning his judgment.

As he watched his parent go off without his breakfast to obtain the services of skidding animals in the harbor village upshore, Aaron knew the time had come. He and Olaf had to gain their father's confidence so they could share in decision-making without jarring the proud man's self-esteem.

Stephan came through the shanty's canvas door flap and looked about, obviously concerned for his middle-aged nephew.

14

"Where is Leander?" Alarm cracked his voice. "Is he sick behind the hemlock?"

Aaron pointed to the beach. "He left for Cedar Forks without his breakfast. I don't know whether he ate a piece of bread or not. I can't figure out why he didn't tell us he was leaving."

"Aaron, I'm getting to be a regular old woman who talks too much. Get Olaf out of bed, but don't wake Bjorn. I must say something to you big boys."

Olaf appeared, asked, "Where's Pa?" then crouched beside the fire Stephan was poking into a cooking blaze.

"Boys," the elderly Norwegian-Dane began, "boys, your papa is out of his mind with sadness and worry. We must do the best we can to help him get his senses together. I can only tell you, unless we get a miracle, your mama is going to be very sick before the summer is over."

Aaron let himself sink onto an overturned fish box they'd used for a chair and Olaf folded to the ground heedlessly close to the pine root fire. Stephan was saying out loud what they'd feared all winter. It was not possible for them to imagine the Johannsen household without the happy and loving presence of their mother, not tolerable to think of the youthful body that had borne them wasted and wracked with agony.

Since Liza and her family had come to Ephraim, he and Bjorn had been sleeping in the heated twine shed. But Liza had told him that his mother slept poorly and prowled about the big kitchen-living room at night, that her time of life had come on hard and fast. What had the doctor told his father? There was only one answer.

Only exuberant Bjorn ate heartily of Stephan's breakfast of steamed eggs and crisp fried potatoes. By good sun they were all in a stand of tall, slim timber on a low ridge behind the clearing. Aaron ax-felled selected straight conifers of suitable diameters for cabin poles. Stephan measured and marked log lengths, Olaf limbed the trunks with his well-honed ax and Bjorn made the saw cuts.

It was disappointing to Aaron that his wartime buddy, Heinie Braun, would not be present for the building construction as they had planned during the winter. Herr Braun had told him bluntly on the last day of his apprenticeship at the cooperage, "You don't help lay up coopershop. You ask make barrel. V'en Heinrich learn fish, he come." Heinie could not be expected to join them till it was time to hang summer-set gill nets in swells of deep water in the bay.

While the rest of the crew took a later nooning, Aaron hewed and bored one of a pair of support bucks to hold the long logs for peeling off the bark. Stephan had gone in the shack to stretch out on his bunk. Six hours of work were more than enough for a sixty-seven-year-old man and another six lay ahead. It was cruel of the Johannsens to expect so much of him, but if he aimed to take unto himself a woman and have a warm, dry home for them both, he'd have to pull his own weight as long as he could. What *had* he promised Garnet in a sudden recurrence of his youth as he'd held a squirming piglet for her to spoon feed?

No matter, it was good that Stephan had found the woman from Tennessee—she'd make a good yokemate for him. It didn't seem like her scrawny body could make much warmth in a man's bed, but she'd heat his socks on the oven door of a cold winter morning and gut his fish when he came off the ice. People could talk all they wanted, but the brown-skinned lady was an unexpected asset to the Johannsen family. She milked the cow when Stephan was gone, she knit nets and fussed over their mother. Whatever Stephan was doing on shore, she followed him, insisting, "You-all go set down—dis here be woman's work."

Aaron pushed an ash sapling leg into a canted hole he'd drilled in a carved cedar buck with a hand auger. He looked around for Bjorn and Olaf; it was time to go back to the woods to work till nightfall. Olaf was stroking his ax with a whetstone and Bjorn could be seen daydreaming on the sunny privy seat with his pants down. It was a shame to disturb him—there were only a few days so early in the spring that you could have such blissful comfort. Then quicker than the eye could register, the boy was buckling his belt and sauntering toward the *Flicka*. What had stung him on the bare bottom side? Sounds of harness jingling and a girl talking!

Knocking on the buck leg with the flat side of his ax head to seat it securely, Aaron went in to get Stephan so he wouldn't be caught resting in the middle of the afternoon. Olaf slid the coffee pot over the hottest coals of their noon fire and checked the bean-pot.

A sightly caravan, walking single file at the edge of the perpetually striving waves, came around the cedar point. Their father, maintaining an upright stance with the aid of a walking stick, stepped ahead of a boy and a girl, each leading a worked down bay horse loaded with bagged oats and hay, rolled blankets, skidding chains and singletrees.

5

A Girl Who Knows Buckwheat from Rye

Leander made a beeline to a block of wood by the cabin wall, lowered himself cautiously to it and sat with his staff between his knees as a brace for his arms and upper body. His right leg was twitching noticeably but he congratulated himself on how closely he had calculated almost the exact distance his sea legs would carry him on land. Since the first light of day, he'd walked and trotted fifteen miles on an Indian trail over every sort of terrain except hills. He'd been in water to his thighs where it had been necessary to cross brooks emerging bankfull into the waters of Green Bay.

He was too weary to talk, but they were all standing there with their mouths open, waiting for an account of his morning's activities. "Well," he began (wouldn't they like to know *all* that had happened to him?), "the blacksmith told me Swanson took his oxen to haul hemlock bark for Spalding. He said where I could find Carl Nicholson. Nicholson hauls freight on the Bay de Noc Road from Menominee. The road is broken up from the thaw. His team has no work for two weeks. I was in luck!"

"I guess you were!" Aaron concurred enthusiastically before he pulled the *Flicka* to the bank, vaulted aboard and searched in the food box for bread and cheese for the latecomers. Stephan took the gelding from the skinny, towheaded boy whose demeanor challenged anyone to think he was a caricature of a man. The girl was about eighteen and undoutedly knew buckwheat from rye.

The Nicholsons' father, a man as old as Stephan, had broken his hip in a fall from a loading dock in January. The girl had quit her job in a boardinghouse and had begun transporting supplies with her brother. Other teamsters had respected a girl who could

18

make her run on time without ganting her horses and a fifteen-year-old bundled-wire boy who kept two smooth throwing stones in his pocket.

Leander felt his wool underwear and pants drying on his legs and he began to itch. He didn't blame the boys for being curious about the Nicholsons, but they'd have to wait for a more private moment to hear the whole story. Those two young people were perfectly capable of getting on their horses and riding back to Cedar Forks if they found the situation unsatisfactory in any way.

The only concession the girl had made to the masculinity of her job had been to cut her Swede-blond hair like a peasant boy's and shorten her skirts to mid-calf. It didn't take brawn to drive horses—some of the best teamsters in the woods were no bigger than jockeys—but loading heavy bundles and crates was another matter. That was where brother-sister teamwork came in.

He'd been so elated at securing the horses that he'd not figured out sleeping arrangements for the night, though he had promised Mrs. Nicholson her children would have safe shelter. On the way from the village the girl, Amanda, or Mandy as she had been called by her father, had said maybe they could stretch a canvas lean-to on the shanty for her and her brother, Gunnar. That had relieved him, but their only hope for adequate sleeping conditions for a bunch of men and a lone young woman was a continuation of the mild weather.

He watched Bjorn move to take the mare's lead rope from the girl. He'd have to keep an eye on that boy—he was at an age when a pretty girl could make a man of him in seconds. She seated herself on Aaron's box and spread her gray skirt to dry. She didn't look out of place in a construction camp, but neither did it seem possible that she could do the tricky footwork required to keep from getting a broken leg while skidding long logs. She was taking in everything about the Johannsens with eyes the color of reedy shallows.

Aaron had given him a quizzical glance when he'd seen the girl from Cedar Forks, but Leander was well aware of his problems. One, how could a girl be explained to Helga and Liza? He could tell them about Gunnar's remarkable accuracy with a rock, but that wouldn't reduce the incontrovertible ratio of six men to one girl.

His second problem was more pressing, the lack of a proper outhouse. The girl would have to eat and drink before three days were up and the woods was too distant for emergencies. She'd dropped behind on the trail, but something had to be done before night. The boys believed he'd lost his grip on things—he could see that more and more each day. But he'd bet they'd not have thought of that part of Mandy Nicholson's comfort.

The prospect of old age scared him out of his mind; he'd come from a line of men who'd lived to interminable senility. Now, verging on that age, he held himself as much as he could from emotional decisions and forgetfulness; but lately it seemed the harder he tried, the less he succeeded.

He stood on his feet and began to move about lest stiffening legs cause him to walk like a doddering old man. Olaf had served Mandy and Gunnar their lunch; now he offered him a plate of food. He took it and beckoned Stephan to follow him in the shack. Inside, reclining on an elbow, he gestured to his uncle with his fork and directed, "Bjorn will get you a jib sail out of the *Flicka* before we go to the woods to skid. You set four posts around the privy hole and wrap the jib around them. Then you make the boy and girl a tent from the front of this shed with one of the tarps. When you're done, you can cook us a good supper."

But Leander could tell his uncle had not been fooled. "My boy," Stephan returned, "you couldn't crawl to the woods on your hands and knees after that walk. I'll help skid and *you* make the tent—when you can get out of bed."

6

The Built-up Shoe

The next afternoon spring abandoned them. In the woods Aaron felt it go as he threw aside limbs from a previously skidded tree to make a short new trail for Mandy Nicholson's mare, Gert. Gunnar and Mandy each had a skid remaining for their horses and their second day of work would be ended, a hard day with bruises, scratches and broken harness.

Olaf had taken some coffee and bread to the timber with him that morning and had not come out all day. Aaron knew his older brother felt his task of chopping out snagging roots and lifting away the limbings and dead wood made his gimpy leg less conspicuous than working in the clearing. Bjorn peeled and skidded logs at the building site while Stephan and their father hewed joists and stringers. Olaf had asked specifically that, of the two Nicholsons, Gunnar be sent to work on his skidway, but his eyes had followed Mandy as she moved about the camp the evening before.

Watching Mandy and Gunnar work, earning their living the hard way, Aaron was more aggravated with his father than he'd ever been. How could a person in his right mind employ a girl and a boy on a risky job that had put many a woodsman in leg splints for the winter?

"I'll take this last log out of your trail and finish up Olaf's skidway on my next trip," Mandy told him as she returned to his side of the slashing and backed her horse handily to the butt of a spruce bole. "Gunnar's reversing some logs for your father in the clearing."

Gunnar had been stolidly swaying with fatigue on his last skid from Olaf's cutting and Aaron was relieved that the boy would be in the open where Stephan could look out for him. But Olaf would be disconcerted when Mandy showed up in his skidway. Olaf was twenty-seven, old enough to cope for two minutes with a bone-weary, grimy slip of a girl, but he'd been mumbly and bumbly when Mandy'd come within six feet of him the night before.

After Mandy left with his log, Aaron hacked his way out the back of the working area and cruised around through a mixed stand of tall evergreen trees, blazing selections to be cut the next morning. He chopped through a deadfall, acutely aware that the sound of his ax was reverberating there for the first time since the earth was set in orbit. He limbed several straight balsam firs as high as he could reach and the scent of their sap surrounded him. On a small hummock the size of a room, dead evergreen needles and prince's pine were padded down and piles of drummels littered the edges. Deer had bedded there during the night; the does would be heavy with fawn now.

Aaron could hear Olaf working off to the south across a haphazard windrow of tree tops, limbs and debris. He had been about to make his way around the aromatic pile of discards when the sound of harness alerted him that Mandy was bringing her horse into Olaf's skidway. He slowed his pace and made dead limbs crack with his ax, but Olaf heard neither him nor the oncoming horse. Lost in his work or some sort of daydream, he bent with a swooping movement and picked up a frond of pungent arborvitae cedar with its exquisitely flattened and connected needles, then he threw it away and pried an unwanted tree top out of the trail.

A horse appeared and Olaf saw that Mandy had replaced Gunnar. Panic flashed over his face, but the rapid approach of the girl shook him back into the reality of the situation.

Aaron restrained an instinctive impulse to join his brother and smooth things for him. No, Olaf had spent sixteen diligent years cultivating a shell of reserve that he was going to have to shuck right now. Their father had inadvertently found a girl his bachelor son could not avoid with devious excuses. She was here, a girl who, from all indications, Olaf had been instantly ready to work for, die for and raise a family with.

The bay mare, still brisk and springy after a long day, followed Mandy like a dog. The horse dragged an ironwood single-tree by one trace. A logging chain attached to it snaked through the uprooted leaf mold and forest duff. Holding an arm out to indicate her intention to the mare, the girl halted and explained quickly to Olaf, "Your father has Gunnar moving some logs into place for his house. Is this cedar the last log you want taken out of here?"

Shifting most of his weight on his good leg and using his ax as a cane to level his body, Olaf acknowledged the questioning wave of her hand with a confirming one of his own. Mandy hooked the free end of the singletree to its trace and drew on the skidding chain to signal the mare to back into position three feet from the end of the log. Stooping, guarding her dangling skirts, she detached the chain and handed the round hook to Olaf. "Here, you chain the log. You can do it better than I can."

When Olaf had done that, Mandy took up the slack and slipped a link of the chain into a grab hook hanging from a clevis on the singletree.

Fearing he would snap a twig if he attempted to retreat from what he knew now was an intrusion, Aaron leaned back against a hemlock in the background.

It was unbelievable but Olaf was speaking easily to the girl. "Isn't that your jacket on the horse's hame?" he asked her. "I'll get it for you. It's getting colder by the minute."

Mandy's gray wool smock had long bloused sleeves accentuating the girlishness of her wrists, but it was thin and had been pushed through at the elbows by the strenuousness of her activity.

As Olaf walked around the off side of the mare to fetch the coat, Aaron knew his brother was willing the girl to see that his defect had not dimished his vigor. If only Olaf had not favored his leg when it had hurt him so badly as a boy in Denmark. He'd been growing so fast, by the time he'd discarded his crutch, his good leg had increased an inch in growth over his indulged one.

Watching Olaf hold the garment for Mandy, Aaron thought: Well, at least there's no way for the Swede girl to know yet that she's made a whole man of Olaf.

Pointing to the long reins looped from a harness surcingle ring, Olaf perservered, "Do you want the lines to drive the mare with or will you lead her?"

Mandy smiled, showing the strong, slightly curving teeth that often go with dimpling cheeks. "Gert'll follow me out of the brush on her own. I'll drive her when we get to the field."

"I'll come out of the woods behind you—it's long past quitting time."

"Olaf?" The girl's tentative tone was a prelude to something. "Olaf, my father was a cobbler and a harness maker in Sweden. You must let him make a built-up shoe for you."

It was a stunning and disturbing statement but Mandy's face showed she meant it in kindness and concern. She'd had to speak now—there'd be no opportunity at all back in camp. Would Olaf clam up in anger and resentment just as things were going good for him?

"No," he was replying with no awkwardness, "I had one when we lived in Denmark, but my father thought it was bad for my good leg."

"You're a grown man now; it'll work, you'll see."

"Well now," Olaf answered with unexpected spirit, "if you're giving advice, maybe you won't mind taking some—you should wear a man's clothes if you're going to do a man's work. That skirt is a trap in the woods."

Good for Olaf!

Mandy held the soiled and torn hem of her dress for Olaf's inspection. "You're right! You wouldn't believe how much trouble this skirt has been for me today."

She turned, spoke to the mare then leaped out and ran ahead in the skidway. The horse set her legs and hauled the thirty-foot-long piece of timber toward the path's exit on the clearing.

Watching the skidder go, Olaf seemed so appalled at all the talking he'd done that he nearly neglected to jump when the small end of the log was catapulted sideways as the horse made a bearing turn around a stump.

Aaron retraced the blazing he'd made through the timber and came out of the woods on his own trail.

7

Walk On the Waves Like Jesus

Leander watched Olaf watch Mandy as they all sat around a twilight fire. Except for the girl, they'd each gone down to the bay to wash personal supper utensils. She'd suggested in a most ordinary way to Olaf, "Would you take mine with yours, please? I'll help your Uncle Stephan clean the pans and put the food away."

What could have happened between those two in the cabin pole slashing at the edge of the trackless forest? Mandy had been in Olaf's skidway only long enough to chain up a log and come out again. In that short space of time a secret relationship had come into being.

The beechwood fire warmed the angle made by the Nicholsons' lean-to canvas shelter and the log cabin. Aaron and the boy had skid enough dry hardwood the afternoon before to keep several night fires. Tonight's flames flickered higher than the shack and snatched at Stephan's improvised clothesline in isolated gusts of wind. The *Silver Guld* strained toward the mouth of the brook, her mooring line taut. Somewhere in the arctic regions north of Lake Superior weather was brewing.

"The way the skies look tonight, we'll be lucky to have time to cut and skid a few hemlock dock timbers tomorrow morning before we leave for home," Leander said to the group in general.

"We can't take the *Flicka* across the bay in a real blow," Aaron was quick to remind him. "We have to remember what's happened to fishermen who've tried to sail Stahl boats in heavy wind and sea. The *Flicka's* no foul weather craft."

Leander chose to ignore Aaron's remarks. "We'll have Gunnar and Mandy back on that old Indian trail before noon and we'll

25

be gone ourselves." With that, the weariness of the day and the warmth of the fire lulled him into a reverie.

Here in this clearing his American dream would come true. Here he would be patriarch of his own clan, living to a venerable old age with a keen interest in his fishermen grandsons. In the mesmerizing flames he could see Olaf's and Stephan's homes on the south side of the creek together with the transitory outline of Henning's cottage in the margin of the woods. On the north side of the stream he and Aaron would have their families with space for a house for Bjorn when the time came.

Suddenly he was driven to spring up, retrieve the blanket from his shoulders and go in to his bunk to be alone. How could he have daydreamed away Helga's illness?

The next day, in spite of having lived with the lakes country's mercurial weather for a decade, Leander was surprised and confused by the abruptness of the turbulence that came before eleven o'clock. Strong bursts of wind were followed almost immediately by driven hail. As he observed the rolling, roiling clouds racing to the southwest, he fervently wished they'd gone home the day before when the weather was calm. Further, he bitterly resented nature's tricking him into poor judgment.

Everyone had been working so hard and fast that obvious atmospheric signs had escaped them. Aaron and Gunnar had skid hemlock logs on the far side of the creek, and he and Stephan had hewed them for stringers for a bridge across the waterway to the location of Stephan's future house and the cooperage. Olaf had set dock pilings with a drop hammer while Mandy tidied the camp and made the Nicholson belongings ready for departure. Bjorn had sawed and split a good store of firewood.

A blast of hail expanding into snow obliterated the woods and Mandy's mare turned her tail to the storm. Leander knew he should have sent the Nicholsons home. There was no shelter for their valuable horses and he would no more abuse another man's beasts than his own. Then, as unexpectedly as it began, the wind and precipitation subsided and the sun shone coldly. If they set sail that very moment, they could tack a safe distance south of Whaleback Shoal and keep their promise to the Johannsen women that they'd be home by evening. The Nicholsons could be safe in the Forks in little more than an hour if they rode the horses.

Aaron had accompanied Gunnar out of his cutting with a long tree trunk swerving behind the horse. It was clear the two were discussing something as they unhitched the horse from the log. Aaron kept looking at the northeastern sky and when Leander followed suit, he was shocked to see how things had worsened in a few minutes. Gunnar swung onto the horse and kicked him down into the creek and across to the campsite while Aaron walked over the bridge timbers with the chain and singletree.

"We've got to get Mandy and Gunnar on the trail!" Aaron shouted against the sounds of the sea and Olaf's drop hammer.

Leander started to the *Flicka* with his broadax. "Aye," he agreed, "it's going to snow again. We'll move out right now."

He stepped closer to Olaf. "You let that go and help Mandy," he directed as his son began dismantling the pile driver. "I'll give Bjorn a hand to put our gear in the boats."

"Wait a minute!" Aaron broke in, holding an angrily deterring hand to his youngest brother as he spoke. "We'll have Mandy and Gunnar off as soon as we can, but we stay right here."

Leander felt rage and frustration rise like bile. "I told your Mama I'd come home today and I will. What are you talking about, stay?"

"Take a good look at the way the *Guld* is pitching. Did you see that horizon a few minutes ago? There's waves out there as high as a house."

Was Aaron implying that his father was incapable of rational decisions?

Again the sun was obscured and a sheet of icy, wind-borne rain forced them to turn their faces. Aaron helped Olaf ready Mandy's horse and Olaf lifted her to a seat behind the hames and surcingle of the harness. It came to Leander's mind that Olaf, at least, had not tried to defy his father. Then he distinctly heard Olaf say to the girl, "I'll come and see your father as soon as I can." Now what did that mean? Something was afoot. Olaf was a good boy—what had happened?

"Goodby," Olaf told the girl. "Look out that your horse doesn't stumble." The skidders rode along the brook bank and around the clump of aspen to the beach with a businesslike jangle of harness.

The rain was changing to snow again as they last glimpsed the riders trotting into the blizzard. Mandy's skirts flew up and Leander noted with relief that she wore long underwear.

Aaron, Stephan and Bjorn had gone into the bunkhouse, but Olaf lingered, his eyes fixed on the sandy point where the Nicholsons had vanished.

"Carl Nicholson has good horses," Leander said, seeking to cheer his son. "They'll go right to their barn in no time."

"I don't know," Olaf worried, "that old trail wanders. You said yourself it has confusing branches. There's no way we can know for sure, any time soon, if they make it home safely."

That uncertainty also deeply concerned Leander. Allowing the young people to ride off into a northeaster could turn out to be a ghastly mistake on his part. But if they had stayed at the camp where there was no cover for the horses and the animals had taken distemper and died, that would have been his fault too.

"When we come back from Ephraim, you can sail the *Flicka* to The Forks and pay Carl Nicholson the rest I owe him for the use of the horses," he told Olaf, attempting to reassure his son as they bucked the gale to the shack.

Inside the inadequate structure, he raised the already flapping canvas roof by announcing to his sons and uncle, "Now we will go home to Mama."

Aaron swung his feet to the dirt floor and stood in an attitude of anger and exasperation beside his vacated bunk. "What's the matter with you?" he shouted. "That storm's only beginning."

Leander knew it was a futile test of his authority but he argued anyway, "If it's only a squall or two—it'll blow over by the time we get the boats loaded."

"No." Aaron stood his ground. "You and I have families to think of, and the way it looks, Olaf and Uncle Stephan have ideas too. And you're not going to take Bjorn out and dump him in the drink or let him be wrecked on the island. I say we stay here till morning. One more night won't matter in the end."

"Matter?" Leander knew Aaron was right but he felt dazed and dogged. "The matter is, Mama will be sick with worry if we don't get home on time. I'll keep my promise and go in the *Guld*. She can take any weather."

Aaron softened. "Pa, I know what you're anxious about. We're all upset about Ma, but we don't want her to see our battered bodies carried off the beach."

Olaf was restless, and Leander saw that his oldest son was inclined to agree with his brother. "I think Aaron's right this time," he remarked quietly. "We have plenty of food and firewood. The way that cold's coming in, the wind'll lay by morning. It's storming in Ephraim the same as it is here. Ma'll know we can't come home."

"If we wait till morning, we'll have ice in our boats," a stubborn bent in Leander made him persist.

"It'll melt when the sun comes up," Olaf said, persuading gently. It eased Leander's mind a little to have someone concerned for his inner turmoil. But it was hard to comprehend that Aaron, in saying they were not to take the boats out on the water this day for any reason, was making clear that *he* was the captain from now on.

Well, if he couldn't take one of the boats to go home to Helga, when he got a chance, he'd start off walking on the waves like Jesus.

Stephan stood up and looked out the small window. "There's too many good men and boats at the bottom of that water now," he said. "I stay here."

Then Bjorn offered his opinion, "I saw those two sailors who washed ashore after the *Dudley Barnes* went down with a load of lumber when I was thirteen. I don't want someone to take my naked body away from the ravens next July."

The tenseness of the last half hour had shut off Leander's circulation. He had to go outdoors where he could move about and breathe. Two rods from the bunkhouse door the *Liten Flicka*, safe from the brunt of the storm, was tossing rhythmically. He had an almost irrepressible urge to board the lithe boat, lie on her bottom, cover himself with a tarp and let her rock him into oblivion. But he must see to the larger boat, the *Silver Guld*. The wind was catching her squarely and there were rocks too close to her stern.

As he had feared, the *Guld* was fishtailing toward a boulder that stuck out of the water like a petrified stump. Where were those lazy boys? Didn't they know that their most dependable craft, the boat he and Stephan had built from standing tree to sail, would soon have a hole in her the size of a fish barrel?

8

Yank Up the Centerboard

"You know, all during the war, I never wanted to be at home in Ephraim as bad as I do right now in this storm." Aaron spoke to his brothers and granduncle in the unheated shed where they sat freezing and talking to pass the time. "I always used to enjoy an April blizzard when everyone was ashore and accounted for and Ma baked us special treats in the hearth oven. But this one makes me feel like the time a squad of Rebs caught our platoon fording a flash-flooded creek in Tennessee just after Henning was killed. Some of us were on one side, some on the other—nobody knew what to do or where to go."

Bjorn, demonstrating that he was a man with a man's thoughts, quipped, "Now I wonder why your heart is all of a sudden in Ephraim? Have you just realized that Liza is a good-looking woman and ought not to be let out of your sight?"

Olaf rose from his seat on the food chest that had been brought in from the *Flicka* and added a serious dimension to the conversation, "Have we forgot? Pa's still down by the *Guld*. He's afraid of those rocks on her port. I think I'd better go out and see what he's doing."

Aaron jumped up from the boot locker. "No, I'll go. You see what's left in the grub box. I was going anyway." He pulled back the door flap and shivered. "Well," he said, "there's only one thing good about this weather—it's too cold to snow much longer."

His ten years younger brother Bjorn also sat on the locker. Now he hugged himself and pretended to shake from the cold. "C-couldn't we c-cut a hole in that canvas roof and build a tepee fire in here?"

"We'll be lucky if the wind don't crack that frozen tarp or blow it off, the way it is," Stephan reminded him. "If we open it up, the whole thing will go and we *will* freeze to death."

Aaron was more than ever disgusted with himself for not noticing that the fishing shanty heater had been left in the twine shed back on the peninsula. Their father had promised he'd take care of loading it but had absently neglected the chore. Though he had no stomach for it, Aaron knew this was the turning point— someone would have to be alert about monitoring fishery activities from now on and it would have to be him.

"What do you think you're doing in here?" Their father ducked under Aaron's arm and came through the flap. His shoulders and cap were crusted with icy snow and he'd worked up a barely controlled fury to relieve his tension. "You all sit there like crows in a dead tree and let the *Guld* break up on the rocks. I'll go myself. I'll put my boots on and I'll beach her. "Get up!" he brushed Bjorn from the longboot container. "I'll go myself," he repeated and extricated his chest-high leather footgear.

Aaron reached into the Danish sea trunk for his own waders. "No, Pa, I'll go. I was on my way to see what you thought when you came in the door." Then to the rest, "You all come out and be ready to lay all the heft you have on that mooring rope. I'll go aboard the *Guld* and give her some sail. We'll get her up on the beach as far as we can."

"Her flat bottom'll make her stable enough aground," Olaf said, adding ruefully, "it'll take some winching to float her tomorrow, but she'll be seaworthy for the trip home."

When all of the men were out of the shelter, Aaron walked with slapping boots down the creek bank and around the windbent aspens to the *Guld's* mooring post. With visibility foreshortened by the driving snow, he narrowly missed a brink where the voracious sea had undercut and washed away a chunk of dune. He gripped the mooring line with his left hand and waited for a breaker to roll up, divide around the boat and overflow a fringe of grasses, reeds and juniper well up on the shore. He moved along the rope and was instantly in water to his waist. The *Guld* was plunging and straining toward the rocks and a sandbar to her leeward.

It was a good thing their father had been wise enough to insist on anchoring the boat some distance from the mouth of the stream where the beach had no cutbank. The wind seized his breath and the snow plastered his eyes shut as he worked his way through the heaving surf to the bow of the twenty-four-foot craft. The water was intensely cold, only a few degrees above freezing. No man could live in it for long.

Aaron grasped the gunwale and overhanded until he could scramble aboard. Gear was floating in the slush in the bottom of the boat, and the mast was screeching. The wooden vessel was almost defenseless against the pounding of the incalculably mighty sea. He hauled in the anchor, yanked up the centerboard, set the reluctant, half-frozen sail and grabbed a long sculling oar.

The mainsail bellied, the *Silver Guld* lunged like a spooked horse and was solidly aground.

He heard the men on shore shouting congratulations as he took in sail. He sat then for a moment on a net box with his face averted from the snowy gale. There was all the time in the world now. When he vaulted ashore, his feet would be out of the reach of the rampaging bay. Sitting there, he surprised himself with an admission. Four years of living and fighting in the Southland had changed his daredevil attitude toward the water. From now on he would have more respect for the power and the accident provoking caprices of the freshwater sea on which they made their living.

As the temperature fell, the snow tapered off and the wind, relieved of its burden, increased in velocity. They all went out and scooped the freezing slush from the boats; then for an hour they applied their collective minds to the problem of procurring comfort for the night. They still craved the primitive benefit of fire in their abode.

Finally Stephan reiterated his original idea, "I tell you, we should take the two-man saw and cut a big door in the front of the shack and bring our fire in close. We'll leave a sill log and cover it with wet sand."

"By George! that's what we're going to do." Aaron got to his feet and gave the older man an approving hug. "It won't make us any colder."

"While you boys do that, I'll make us some biscuits and bacon and eggs. Our women packed us plenty."

Aaron smiled at his granduncle's designation of "our women". He'd never mentioned that he might marry Garnet. Did he really plan on setting up housekeeping with her? The fact that Garnet was half Negro meant he *must* go before a clergyman with her as a matter of special regard.

9

Indians in the Turbulent Night

The carefully laid new fire blazed before the six-foot-wide doorway. Five o'clock came and they were sitting in the cave-like shelter drinking coffee and eating Stephan's satisfying supper. Leander looked out at the *Liten Flicka*, buffeted but secure in the creek. By their own cunning, they had outwitted the elements. It was good for five men of one blood to sit together on a cold evening, sated and almost warm, and talk of how best to deal with the great water that gave them their livelihood. And it was a blessing that the nets were still safe in the boxes back in Ephraim—the storm would have blown them out had they been set.

For half an hour Leander filled his thoughts with comforting fantasies of his life as it might have been on the Michigan side of the bay if things had gone as he had planned. He was sedated by dreams when something abruptly caused him to look up. How long had Helga, Liza, Garnet and Naomi been standing there on the far side of the brook? Live voices had drawn him from his mental retreat and he jumped up crying, "They're here! They're here!" before he could stop himself.

Aaron looked up, confused. "Who? What are you talking about?"

Then they all saw the shawled, huddled group on the south end of the half-built bridge. Nine visitors, a flurry of wind-blown buckskin tatters, were gesticulating and debating. A baby wailed and an elderly couple swayed in the arctic blasts of the gale. Two young children pulled their mother's skirts around their raggedly clad bodies.

"Indians," Bjorn said, rising and straightening himself to the intimidating height of an adult male. "We're camped right on their trail."

"We can't leave those women and children out there in the cold." Leander rose from his seat on a net box. "I'll go and get them to the fire." He was still struggling to accept the fact that these were not the Johannsen women, miraculously appeared.

"Wait, Pa. Let me go." Aaron leaped to his feet, objecting.

"No, I will. They'll talk better to an old man." Holding his collar to shield a nagging eyetooth from the fierce wind, he walked to the creek span. Then he was across the hewed sleepers and face to face with strangers who had every moral right to be on Johannsen land. Now what did he say? Thinking wasn't always the best thing at such a time—instinct was a more reliable instructor. He made a courtly gesture of welcome and motioned the Indians to come over the bridge to the fire.

The shorter of the two young men repeated, "Potawatomi, Potawatomi, go to Cedar River."

Leander had heard about the Indian tribe in Sturgeon Bay and knew these people were from a wandering band of a tragically fragmented nation. The United States Government had attempted to forcibly exile the Potawatomi from an area near Chicago to a place called Kansas on the open prairie. A remnant had escaped by pony and canoe. Over a period of thirty years, they'd drifted slowly up the western shore of Lake Michigan to a permanent camp a day's journey up the Big Cedar River from Cedar Forks.

With a few words of English, the Indians said they'd been on their way to join the Cedar River Potawatomi when the bay had become so rough they'd had to beach their dugout canoes and proceed on foot. Leander nodded his head as they talked and his interest pleased them. It was good that he'd taken pains to really listen to the Potawatomi story when it had been related to him.

The fur-swaddled baby began to mewl again with the insistence of a cold, wet kitten with diarrhea. His mother said something to her husband which Leander interpreted to mean, "I go: I sit by the fire and clean and feed my baby." Evidently the rest agreed for they picked up their bundles and the two little girls and followed him to the campfire.

The boys had vacated the warmest seats in the protected doorway and the three women and the children moved with Leander's beckoning hand to the blanket covered boxes. The younger men, approximating Olaf's and Aaron's ages, squatted warily in an attitude of surveillance on the windward side of the fire, well away from the building. They'd thrown back their blankets, revealing front hanging, twin black braids interwoven with buckskin thongs. The older man's thinning gray hair blew in the wind and Leander knew his head was cold.

Stephan shoved the much reheated pot of beans into a nest of glowing coals and stirred cornmeal into the smaller kettle always simmering over the fire. Leander knew most of the Johannsen food supply, intended for four days when packed, had been used up. Would there be sufficient for fourteen people if the storm continued another day?

Well, the Potawatomi were hungry now. There was no knowing how long it had been since they'd last eaten. His own supper lay like a beach stone in his stomach.

He observed their guests without really looking at them and what he saw made him sick and bewildered. How could the same democracy that had promised and given *him* security and even luxury perpetrate the neglect these human beings showed? They were all as thin as white-tailed deer after a yarding winter. The sweet little girls were at the moment cold, hungry, wornout and homeless. His own migration to the New World had been a small cog in the cruel machine that had rolled inexorably over their land, dispossessing and dispersing them.

The older of the two brown-skinned young women laid her baby on the lap of its grandmother then, kneeling, she began to unfold the rabbit fur lined blanket that was the emaciated child's only garment. As she removed the dried sphagnum moss that served as a diaper, Leander's olfactory sense was assailed by an unmistakable odor. Stephan looked up from turning bacon in a skillet and Leander returned his questioning glance. "Do you think it's cholera infantum?" he asked the older man.

The baby's black-eyed father sprang to his feet with a belligerent expression on his even-featured, pock-marked face. "No! No! No choler!" he cried in agitated protest.

Leander was shaken by the reaction to his term and fervently wished it back. How could he explain that he meant uncontrolled diarrhea which, from whatever cause, was as deadly to the very young child as the dreaded Asiatic disease? That infection had been brought sporadically to the midwest by European immigrants, decimating already hard pressed new colonies. Native Americans were rightly terrified of the word.

The Potawatomi were all searching his face, waiting for his reply. Well, if they knew the meaning of the word "no", he would repeat it. "No, no," he reassured them. "Bellyache, bellyache. We'll make medicine for the baby. Medicine." The young Potawatomi went to his son, felt of his small head and nodded acquiescence. The baby undoubtedly had a fever from an influenza picked up in one of the settlements on the route of their journey.

Garnet had sent packets of powder to be mixed with hot water and sugar if any of them came down with the grippe accompanied by symptoms of flux. Stephan had said it was a simple herb remedy. The baby was dying from lack of fluid in his tissues. Leander remembered when Olaf had been so afflicted in the Old Country. The mother rewrapped the child and turned aside to put it to the breast, but the little one, too weak or too sick to nurse, threw its head and whimpered.

Leander took note of the knives in the belts of all three of the male visitors and the solemn faces of his own sons. He saw that Stephan was boiling water for coffee. Taking a clean cupful of the water and a silver spoon, he went to the food chest for the medicine and sugar. There he mixed, tasted and cooled until the resulting infusion seemed strong but not too strong or too hot. The smell of the mint was accentuated by the wind and the heat of the fire.

When he took the cup of liquid to the mother of the baby, she shook her head and looked around, beseeching the old woman for advice. The grandmother took the cup from him and, sipping thoughtfully, smacked her lips to sharpen her taste and began to spoon the potion into the infant's mouth. At first he whined and refused. She dipped her finger in the sweet liquid and introduced it to his tongue. Then the spoon again. Thank God! He was swallowing spoonful after spoonful of the life preserving fluid.

By two o'clock in the morning, the cautiously integrated camp was hushed and almost warm. The obstreperous wind had abandoned its assault on Aaron's Creek, and the stressful snapping of the canvas roof and lean-to had subsided. Even the small Potawatomi boy, after several dosings of Garnet's remedy, had fallen asleep cuddled in the curve of his mother's blanketed body on the ground just inside the cabin doorway.

Aaron and the baby's father kept the pre-morning fire watch. The only sounds were the crackling of the blaze, the breaking of waves and the answering snores of Stephan and the old man.

Leander knew his body needed the refreshment of even two hours of sound sleep and his mind yearned to be still. What then was keeping him so intensely awake? The Indians weren't going to hurt anybody. Someone was talking to him, asking, "Leander Johannsen, who stilled the storm and soothed the child? Who truly is master of the sea and seafarers, of life and death? Who will uphold you when at last your strength is gone?"

Why couldn't he just reply, "You, God, my Father," and go to sleep?

He should have known his refusal to answer the tender voice would be an invitation to another, neither still nor small, "My friend, escape the certain agony of the coming months by sending your crew home without you. Start walking into the wilderness out back. Keep going and hide from pain and death. Confound God. Deprive Him of the pleasure of seeing you writhe, helpless at the sight and sound of your wife's anguish."

Leander flung the blankets from his fully clothed body and stumbled out to sit by Aaron at the fire where the flames would drive back the owner of the nightmare voice.

Aaron put a hot cup of coffee in his trembling hand and asked, "Are you sick, Pa? Can't you sleep?" Then he laid a sympathetic arm about his father's shoulders.

How good it was to have a son who loved him! Feeling the warmth of Aaron's body, he suddenly remembered a few words he'd learned from the Bible a long time ago, *"This is My beloved Son, in whom I am well pleased."* Now he knew that to be an exemplary father to his own much loved sons, he must expect to be an acceptable son to the Father of mankind. But there was more he must do, much more, as Helga had told him many times—though it could not have been easy for her to reason with a bullhead.

Aaron spoke again, "Are you all right, Pa?"

"I'm fine," he said, "I think I just came to my senses and it feels good." As far as he could tell, the worst of the ten-year battle was over. In a few minutes he would go back to bed and sleep.

In the morning he would arise and sail to Ephraim. And on the Sabbath he would take Helga to the little Moravian church at the harbor there. His consistent and convenient excuse that he had been raised a rigid Lutheran and would be guilty of heresy if he worshipped with the Iversen Moravians no longer held water. He remembered Helga had said, "Leander, when you meet God, He's not going to ask you if you are a good Lutheran or a good anything else. He's going to say, 'Leander Johannsen, do you love Me?' "

Helga had steadfastly maintained through the years that the

simplicity and friendliness of the Moravians pleased and satisfied her. They closed their doors or communion table to no worshipper because of secular beliefs or national background. How could he have been offended by their stand that the Bible was the only source of doctrine, that the Lord's Supper should be received in faith and repentance as defined by the New Testament, that godly living was the evidence of a saving faith?

Why had he ignored the hand of brotherhood so often extended to him by members of the congregation who were Scandinavian farmers and fishermen like himself? These men had known pain and bereavement and could, with God's help, bear him up in his tribulation. These were the men who would, at last, carry Helga up the hill to the new cemetery overlooking Ephraim harbor and who would comfort him on the way down with silence and a handclasp.

Yes, he would go home to Ephraim a changed man. Now he knew why the doctor had been so blunt about the nature of Helga's illness—he'd been prodding them to extract ten years of happiness from the one left. God! The year was already half gone! Somehow he must keep himself humble and make the remaining time a foretaste of Heaven for Helga.

He lay on his stomach on his bunk and silently repeated the Lord's Prayer. The hovering love of God warmed him and he fell asleep.

10

Cowshed Nuptials

The *Liten Flicka* rode easily into Ephraim harbor on this, the fairest of spring Sabbath Days. It was now the third weekend that Aaron's father had said on a Saturday evening, "Well, tomorrow we'll all go to church with Mama."

Liza knew Helga had long ago ceased asking her husband to accompany her to the Norwegian colony's chapel on the isolated peninsula. What had happened? Why had Papa Johannsen changed his mind? Had he been stricken with an attack of guilt? Remorse was a driving thing. Were indications of the multiplying seeds of death in his wife's body reminders of his own mortal shortcomings?

As she traveled churchward in the boat with Aaron and his parents, Liza could see the rest of the family of nine, now and then, rolling in the wagon across openings in the brush along the beach. Naomi sat between Garnet and Stephan on the driver's seat while Bjorn and Olaf dangled their legs from the tailgate. It would be a mercy if Stephan didn't fall under the wheels. It wasn't every day a man of his age asked a preacher to perform his first wedding ceremony.

Bundled against zephyrs that would have been warm except they'd passed over chilled waters, she was surprised at how pleasant it was to be rocked in the cradle of the deep when the bay was in an obliging mood. The *Flicka's* smell of a cleaned up fishing boat had not offended her, but she kept her eyes off the water and concentrated on landfall. Yet, when she soberly considered the terrifying depths under the thin hull of the craft, she became lightheaded and momentarily uncertain about marrying a man who was already wedded to a keg of whitefish.

She glanced at the gentian-eyed woman who sat wrapped in a heavy gray shawl on a blanket-padded box by the port gunwale. Deep happiness shone in Helga's eyes. This was the day when Aaron was to make arrangements with Pastor J. J. Groenfeldt for the two weddings that would be held in the Johannsen home the first Sunday afternoon in June.

Though Liza cared for Aaron and needed to be with him with an urgency that increased daily, she had also fallen in love with his mother. There was an ineffable kinship between them that transcended words. Why did this mutual feeling flourish like the gardens of Heaven when the numbered days were dwindling?

Helga's happiness lit and lifted her household, and when intractable pain overtook her, she went into her bedroom and shut the door. At these times Garnet would follow her with hot, flannel wrapped plates and a steaming cup of tea, brewed sometimes from her store of mountain herbs and often from the packets of powders a doctor had sent from Green Bay. Presently in a still moment, Garnet could be heard reading Helga's choice of Scriptures.

One day, the door ajar, Liza realized Helga was teaching Garnet the Twenty-third Psalm in a new language, probably Swedish; but another time she detected the spellbinding cadence of an African chant. Back in the southern hills Norris Peake's father had whipped Garnet when she'd sung like that to Liza's mother-in-law as she lingered with an illness similar to Helga's. Leander would also be furious if he heard the half-Negro woman, but Mama Johannsen was often asleep after one of Garnet's incantations.

In the boat, Helga gave her a speaking smile and Liza remembered some of the things her hostess had told her. "You'll have to name your first baby boy Simon Peter after Aaron's grandfather," she'd teased gently. "He carved the rocking crib all our children used and it would have served our grandchildren too—if Leander had not been so stubborn about bringing it along. He could have taken it apart and brought it in the big sea chest, but he said, no, we could only take the boat building tools and whatever else we *had* to have."

"Didn't you come across the water on a big boat?" Liza asked.

"The *Ocean Bird*, the clipper we sailed on from Denmark, was narrow beamed and fast," Helga explained, "but her master was particular about excess baggage."

Within reach of Aaron where he stood at the tiller, Liza faced forward, looking past Leander who leaned on the centerboard rack. He was enjoying, as they all were, the view of the new settlement climbing the hill above a fringe of tall-masted sailing craft in the harbor. Now he stepped back and hunkered down by Aaron's mother. Liza knew he hoped it would be easier for his wife to ride in the sailing boat than in the springless wagon.

Any jarring or lurching these days subjected Mama Johannsen to back pain that made it difficult for her to carry on. Though she was losing weight drastically, she felt and looked uncomfortably pregnant. So small and frail now, Aaron's mother's body—how had she ever borne five children? One day Helga told her in the only bitter words Liza had heard her speak, "Oh, God gave me a body to have babies with. But I was scared to death of Leander's determination to go to America and I took advice from a girl in our neighborhood. She was something of a strumpet. After Bjorn was born, I said, no more babies. Maybe God is punishing me now. Leander argued, 'Let the babies come—we'll take them to the New World with us.' What happened to me was not his fault."

Liza had sought to comfort her almost mother-in-law. "Hain't ary preacher read you the words, 'Whom the Lord loveth, He chasteneth?' "

Now, wearing a green wool suit and a matching velvet bonnet, she sat on an overturned fish box in the rocking boat. She felt as demure and pretty as any young lady, but the minute she opened her mouth the whole effect would be spoiled. Words were dammed up behind her hillbilly tongue and the more anxious she was to talk to Helga or Aaron, the more she reverted to what all the Johannsens must have considered to be gibberish. How had these people from foreign lands learned to speak English so well in only ten years?

For Aaron's sake, she would have to try harder to speak as his family did.

On the hill to the right and back of the small church on the shore, a young maple had been left to guard a new cemetery. There, before she would really get to know her, Aaron's mama would lie, though her sunny-natured middle child would never rest beside her. Henning was buried in the Southland while she, Liza, the girl from Tennessee, would one day lie in his grave spot or near it.

Few of the original forest trees had been left around the homes of the Norwegian colonists, but young orchards, dooryard shrubs and shade trees would in time clothe the hillside premises in beauty. The steepest bluffs on either side of the harbor were hung with evergreen trees and tapestried with myriad shades of leafing hardwoods.

Dressed in black Sunday best, the suit that would be his marriage garment, Aaron took in the sails and began sculling the *Flicka* to a berth at the sand-backed pilings at the end of the docks. There in the lee of the land the warmth of the day could be felt.

Someone had put an overlarge log on the fire to take the damp from the church and the windows had been opened to let the heat out. Organ and voices, a Watts hymn came sweetly over the water. Though the words were in Norwegian as the service would be, Liza knew the lines and they comforted her in a strange place, *"Jesus shall reign where'er the sun doth his successive journeys run."*

By the light of the small north window of the bedroom, Liza could see that it was nearly six o'clock and time to get up on one's wedding day. Helga was already astir and singing softly in the kitchen, tending something at the stove—boiling one of Stephan's Danish hams by the smell. Naomi was still asleep in the middle of the bed but Garnet's side was empty.

Liza said, "God bless this day," and dressed quickly in her work clothes. Before she left the room, she lifted the sheet that covered her and Garnet's wedding dresses where they hung on the back of the door to look once more at the sweet blue gown Helga had sewed for her. Every stitch had been done by hand with care and love as had the royal purple dress that had been such a surprise for Garnet. Garnet had thought Helga had been making it for herself.

But the grape-colored dress was gone! Liza flashed about, searching the room for the mulatto woman's small carpet valise and the precious shoes she'd shined the afternoon before. They had all been taken from the room along with Garnet's winter coat and boots.

She opened the door into the kitchen and stood there, staring at Aaron's mother, unsure of what had happened or what to say.

"Good morning, Liza. Happy wedding day!" Helga spoke gaily across the big log kitchen and smiled as though this would be a day when pain could be barricaded from joy.

"Mama Johannsen," Liza began, "do you know if Garnet has gone to milk the cow? Did she set her satchel and shoes out here somewhere? Her pretty dress be gone.'' Her voice had gotten away from her and was rising, alerting Aaron's papa who was standing in the doorway of the second bedroom that opened into the kitchen.

"What is going on here?'' he demanded. Can't a man get some sleep on his son's wedding day?''

Liza whirled to return to the chamber she, Garnet and Naomi had been using while the former occupants, Olaf and Stephan, had taken a bed in the open loft above the enclosed sleeping rooms. Leander's brusk manner still flustered her and she nearly always managed to react stupidly, even when he was teasing.

"Wait!'' Leander called her back and this time his tone commanded obedience. "What did I hear you say was missing?''

"I-I can't find Garnet's dress or valise,'' she stammered. Aaron's papa was going to be mad no matter what she said.

"Leander,'' Helga interrupted as she laid thick slices of bacon in a heavy iron spider, "will you please let Liza set the table? We all have something to discuss and we might as well do it while we eat our breakfast.''

Leander jerked his shoulders impatiently and went over and opened the oven door of the range. "Where are the biscuits Garnet's been baking for me when I am home?''

"There aren't any,'' his wife told him. Garnet's not here. You'll just have to eat stove toast with your eggs.''

Now hunger-driven, Olaf came down the loft ladder and Aaron and Bjorn came in from their net shed beds.

"Where is Stephan?'' Leander turned and demanded of Olaf. "Is he sick on his wedding day?''

Liza began to shake and Aaron came over to her at the work cupboard and held her against him. "Uncle Stephan must be in the cowshed,'' he spoke to his father.

"If he is,'' Olaf broke in slowly, "he is wearing his best clothes.''

Leander made the dishes on the table jump as he struck it with a hard blow of his flat hand. "I asked before, what is going on around here? Somebody had better tell me right now!''

"You don't have to worry about milking the cow,'' Bjorn interposed from the chair where he slouched. "I promised Uncle Stephan I would do it.''

Leander advanced on his son. "You've never milked a cow in your life!'' he shouted excitedly. "You will spoil her! That is Stephan's job.''

A knowing look crossed Bjorn's wind-browned face. Right then his secret information made him an equal among adults, even with his intimidating father. "Uncle Stephan went on a long journey," he said, initially telling as little as he had to.

Leander turned Bjorn to the window facing the bay and the outbuildings. "What are you talking about, boy? Where could an old man like that go?"

Liza gripped Aaron's warm hand. Was her new family going to ruin this special day with an argument the first thing in the morning? There had to be a simple explanation for the elderly couple's behavior.

Helga, calmly breaking fresh eggs in a second skillet of hot bacon fat, looked up speculatively at her husband and announced, "I guess that'll be enough eggs. Garnet and Stephan aren't here."

Bjorn slid his words behind those of his mother, "Kate and Buck are gone too, but I'll take care of the rest of the stock, like I promised."

Leander sat down in his captain's chair. His face had the stricken look of a man who'd been tricked by trusted friends. He glanced specifically at his wife and his youngest son. "If somebody doesn't tell me everything," he warned, "I will not eat my breakfast."

Liza knew the possible consequences of that threat. Without a full stomach in the morning, Aaron's father could not be tolerated.

"Sit down everybody. Bjorn and I'll tell you what we know while we eat. Leander, I guess you'll have to say grace." The earlier high spirits were gone from Helga's voice and she dropped into her chair.

Leander bowed his head and repeated stiffly, "Lord, bless this food and this house. We thank you. Amen." Then with the remainder of one breath he commanded, *"Now* tell me."

Bjorn, swallowing the whole yolk of an egg, snatched as much importance as he could from the moment, "Uncle Stephan and Garnet are riding the horses around the bay to Cedar Forks. They've been gone for two hours."

Leander motioned away the platter of eggs Aaron was offering him and stood up. "That is a hundred and seventy miles! The trail is bad. Stephan doesn't know about saddles. He'll wreck the ones we've borrowed from Oliver Nelson."

"You can't hurt old cavalry saddles," Aaron said.

"Garnet knows all about riding horses and mules, you don't have to worry," Bjorn contributed. "She'll take good care of Uncle Stephan and the horses."

"But you and Olaf were supposed to take Buck and Kate in the morning. Everything was ready," his father reminded him coldly as he sat down and served himself a sheaf of fried eggs.

Bjorn attempted to explain, "Olaf and I didn't want to go on the ride, and Uncle Stephan and Garnet didn't want to get married. I thought it would be all right if they took our place. I knew Olaf wouldn't care. He wants to get back and see that Mandy girl in Cedar Forks and the *Flicka* is much quicker for that."

"Not get married?" Leander shoved his plate from him and stormed, "Are they going to sleep in sin alongside the trail at night?"

"I think not," Helga intervened quickly. "They *are* married."

For the first time Liza saw Leander throw a stern look at his wife. "Did they run off to Groenfeldt in the night or did the Lord God, Almighty, marry them in their sleep?" he inquired acidly.

Helga began to explain with care, choosing her words, "Garnet couldn't bring herself to actually stand up in front of a group of people and marry a white man, though she is half white herself. They asked me to come to the barn last night at milking time so they could talk to me. I went in the cowshed with my egg basket and there they were, standing in front of the cow, crying. When I asked them what the matter was, they told me. They wanted to be man and wife, to be able to help and comfort each other; but Garnet had simply panicked about legally marrying a white man in a public ceremony.

"All of a sudden it came to me that they needed a Good Samaritan and it was going to have to be me. I could be God's helper and marry those lovely old people right there."

Leander's face turned gray, accentuating his new summer freckles. "But you are a woman!" he cried.

"Oh, I'm a woman all right!" Helga flung back at him. "I have these big sons to prove it, but that doesn't mean God wouldn't talk to me and tell me what to do. So I told Garnet and Stephan, 'I'll marry you now in this place if you'll kneel and hold hands.' I stood there with my two hands on their heads and I said, 'Dearly beloved, do you promise to cleave to each other and to God as long as you both live and have your right minds?'

"Garnet gripped Stephan's hands tightly in both of hers and

said, 'I promise, Miss Helga.' Stephan got his hands loose, pulled her against his shoulder and said the same thing without the 'Miss'.

"Then I said, 'May God richly bless your life together, Mr. and Mrs. Eckberg;' and they got up and hugged each other. We all cried a little, while the cow lowed for someone to milk her."

Leander had been listening in paralyzed silence to the recounting of his wife's shocking deed, but now he said in a controlled voice as though it was still an unspeakable subject, "Helga, you know it is not legal, what you did."

"Well I'll tell you, Leander," Helga reached up on the table for one of his clamped-together hands and brought it down into her lap where she stroked it with her own, "here in America, in the Cedar Forks wilderness where we'll be, no church warden or town sheriff is going to come to the Eckberg's new home and brand it as a house of adultery."

Liza looked at Aaron's mother with admiration and deepening respect as Helga concluded, "Now I think you'd better finish your breakfasts and let us women do our work if we're going to have fifty people here for supper tonight."

Then an urgent thought crossed Liza's mind; as soon as the men left the room, she'd have to find out about Helga's medicine. How would they manage without Garnet during the week or more it would take the elderly couple to ride around the deep indentation of the bay and the rest of the family to move to Aaron's landing in the fishing boats?

Naomi came in from the bedroom in her nightgown and Aaron took her up on his lap to eat her breakfast. The dark-haired, gray-eyed child smiled around the breakfast table. "Tonight I get to sleep with Mama and Uncle Aaron," she said, watching for the effect of her announcement. "Garnet's going to be in Uncle Stephan's bed. Tomorrow night, I'll be big enough to sleep in my own bunk."

Bjorn chortled and Leander seemed about to scold Naomi. Liza rose from the table and went to the cupboard to prepare a pan of dishwater, standing with her back to the room in embarrassment. It was going to be a long wedding day.

11

A Eunuch in His Own House

Now in June, sailing west between Chambers Island and Whaleback Shoal, the mainland of the northern peninsula of Michigan looked much as it had, viewed in February from the ice. Interwoven with the lighter greens of leafing birch and maple, the dark ribbon of evergreen trees edging the low shoreline was accented with nubs of blooming wild cherry.

The Johannsen clearing was shaped like the unbroken half of a walnut kernel with the stream dividing quarters on which two log buildings each had been erected. Rocking along with sufficient wind on a good summer day, Leander manned the tiller of the slim-hulled *Liten Flicka* and looked past the couch where Helga, Liza and Naomi sat ahead of the centerboard with the white terrier wedged between them. Were the women contemplating, as he was, the attractive wilderness panorama of their new homesite?

Struggling with a cargo of crated hogs and chickens and a firmly stanchioned cow in the flat-bottomed *Silver Guld*, the three boys were a mile behind them. "Can you see your new houses now?" he asked the ladies over the small sounds of sail, wave and creaking mast. "Helga, yours is the one in front, by the crick and close to the bay. The sea will sing you to sleep at night."

Helga turned to face him over net boxes full of cooking utensils, dishes and bedding. She smiled and assured him, "I *am* looking. It is beautiful. I'm storing it all in my mind for I'll have no occasion to see it from here again."

Leander made himself joke, "Oh, yes you will. You can come along when we set nets and drop the centerboard for us." But he knew the circumstances that would attend her return trip to Ephraim.

47

As they progressed to within sculling distance of the sandy beach, the women began to be easier about their journey in the reputably unstable craft. Liza caught his attention and remarked, "Papa Johannsen, that's a powerful stand of trees yonder. Are there bear and catamount critters about?"

"Aye, there is," he told her. "And wolves too, but we'll shut up our pigs and chickens and leave them alone."

"You hear that, Naomi?" Liza impressed on her daughter. "You must always stay in the dooryard and never cross the branch to Garnet's house lessen I be with you."

The child plucked her mother's sleeve. "Where be the red men Uncle Bjorn told me about?"

Helga glanced back at the stern and said, "Yes, Leander, tell us. Have you seen your Potawatomi friends again?"

"We saw Indians paddle around the point in dugout canoes, but they didn't come ashore."

Helga spoke again as she studied the arrangement of the three houses and a net shed the men had constructed. "The country looks like the lowlands of Finland where the big trees have not been cut. I was raised in the forest—it doesn't frighten me."

Though she was speaking lightly, Leander could see that his wife's facial muscles were tightening and he tried to think of something to talk about that would take her mind off her backache. "Carl Nicholson thinks someday there will be a smooth pike running where the Indian path goes along the beach," he commenced. "He says there'll be a fine bridge across our crick. The road'll be graded and packed so a team can trot a heavy load on it. But Aaron is ahead of Nicholson. Aaron says, before he is a real old man, steam drays will run without rails on that highway and haul the fish to market."

"Leander, you don't mean it!" Helga exclaimed, but she had her eyes fixed on the landing and he knew she saw now only a bed, a closed door and Garnet. God! What would they do for an unpredictable number of days without Stephan's gifted spouse?

Now he no longer cared if the old couple was legally wed. He craved only Godspeed for them on their trek. If one of them became sick or a horse came up lame, they might be forced to make slow progress or none at all on rough trails. Why hadn't he thought of it before? In the morning he would send Aaron with the *Liten Flicka* to Herr Braun's cooperage in Menominee. Heinie Braun must be advised that it was time to set summer gill nets.

When he'd done that, Aaron could rent a horse and ride toward Green Bay to meet Stephan and Garnet.

Maybe it wasn't fair to take Aaron away from his honeymoon but with his war experience he was more apt to find the old folks quickly. Aaron and Liza had been acting like long married people since the young widow had come to the Johannsen home late in February. It wasn't nice of him to think of it, but it was possible that Aaron, unable to unwind from a vicious conflict, had pressured Liza. Time would tell.

At times little mattered anymore—if Stephan was an adulterer, if Liza was with child, if Bjorn ran away to sea as he had begun to threaten to do, if Olaf continued to run after that young Mandy Nicholson in the sawmill port on the Big Cedar River, if a schooner fouled the set nets, if the cow went dry or the potato crop failed.

But it was important that they become settled at once, each family in its own house, and that Aaron bring Garnet to them without delay. Garnet looked exactly like the withered-apple-and-cornshuck doll little Naomi had brought from Tennessee. People in town might snicker at her, and he'd even wondered if she smelled "nigger", had been vaguely disappointed to find an elusive odor of herbs and lavender about her, as if a little sack of dried leaves had been sewed in her corset cover.

What did Garnet do that was so soothing to Helga when they were behind the closed door of the bedroom? How could relief come from her pale-palmed, arthritic hands?

Then, squeezing Helga's hand for attention, Naomi said, "Grandma Johannsen, Did ye know you'uns new house be right 'longside a ourn? Ifen I cain't go to Garnet's house, I'll go to yourn."

The pendulum of Leander's emotion began to swing again when Helga responded immediately to the little brown girl, and he saw how much she loved Aaron's stepchild. Somehow he must stop this tacking back and forth from hope to despair so he could physically do the work of two men. Sails furled, he began to pole his craft up the small creek to the timber and piling dock.

Here in this once hopeful place, life would make or break him within a year. If he was not soon able to tap some source of strength other than his own, he would lose all—his hopes, his wife, his authority, his hitherto dynamic health.

He had been almost miraculously renewed by God's power and peace several times during the past two months—once on the night of the encounter with the Potawatomi in the April storm and the Sundays when he'd gone to Groenfeldt's church with Helga and the family. But with the dawn-to-dark labor of erecting four buildings, the gift had vanished. It was said that love conquered all, but they had loved Henning only as you can love a good and gaily responsive young man and they had lost him.

The Johannsen clan had been eight in number when they made the fearful and expectant journey from Denmark a decade before. Now even when the worst had come to pass, with the addition of the Tennessee women, there would still be eight. And the way it looked, his sons would bring forth offspring in this spot; but he would be an old man and see, in ravagement and despair, every procedure of his plans undertaken. A year ago he could have kept his place as captain of his ship. Helga's illness had killed him before his time.

As he tied up the *Flicka* and made ready to help the women onto the dock, Helga said, "I'm starved. Who's going to help me start a cooking fire? I see the frame and stones where Stephan's been holding forth."

A sudden cloud chill had swept the clearing and Leander sensed that Helga was more cold than hungry. Even with the help of a boatload of volunteers from Ephraim at the last minute, the houses were only half finished. There was no heat in any of them and he should not have brought the women until there was, though it was summer. He'd not told Helga yet that a mason, August Greutzmacher, was coming to stay until home chimneys and the important coopering fireplace were laid.

The sun had reappeared, but the perpetually cold water of the lake cooled the area. He would have to tell Aaron to bring some lengths of iron stovepipe from Marinette for it might be two weeks before Greutzmacher had the chimney built for Helga's stove.

"I'll build the fire," he said. "You women go and inspect your homes. Liza and Aaron have the one just up the beach from ours." He watched Naomi and the dog, then Liza and Helga run through the trampled sand and grass to the cellarless cabins, each a roofed rectangle with one big room and two small ones.

Helga stood with her hand on the latch of their cabin door and waited for him. "Are you still strong enough to carry me over the sill?" she teased.

"I'll put you on the bed we moved yesterday and you can rest while I make some hot tea. When the boys get here, we'll have a good supper."

The feather heft of her body shocked him. He laid her on the narrow bed, covered her up and kissed her as he would a child. Only a spark of vivacity was left in the rounded, even buxom, girl he had married. God! He would be alone with her tonight though Olaf and Bjorn would be sleeping in the next room. What could he do for her if pain kept her awake and she paced the floor in the night-cold big room? Olaf! With Garnet God-knew-where and Liza in her own house, he would ask Olaf to stay up with his mother if someone was needed. The oldest of their children, Helga had borne him in great pain; he could comfort her now in the long chilly night hours.

He escaped to his task of firebuilding and to watch the *Guld* bring the boys into the pound boat slip. How could he himself be of so little help to his wife when she had comforted him so sweetly for nearly thirty years? Somehow he'd blamed her for her trouble and subconscious condemnations clumsied his hands and tongue.

It struck him agonizingly then that he would not be plagued with this ineptness had he always loved her more than he loved himself; and he would not this moment be actively coveting the presence of an ex-slave who was probably dawdling in the bushes along the way, coaxing Stephan to do something he was too old to do.

But Stephan was not too old. More than that, with Olaf courting Mandy Nicholson and Aaron newly married, the fishery would be overrun with mating-minded males while his wife's illness emasculated him. He would be a eunuch in his own house.

He slammed the ax into the block of dry cedar kindling wood he was splitting fine for a quick fire. He drove the blade close to his left hand, then closer as the block became a final stub. It would be easy to cut his hand off so, bleeding dangerously, someone would know he was alive. But it wasn't his left hand that needed severing, it was his head. That would cure the cancer that was killing him. Unlike Helga's, his malady was of the spirit, but double-deadly for it ate the whole man.

12

Pale Horse and Rider

Aaron sailed into the mouth of the Menominee River between barges, brigantines and yawls. A wood-fired freighter took on lumber at a sawmill pier and chain-wrapped rafts of rough-sawn boards were being moved to schooners anchored in the bay. He'd winch the *Flicka* aground at Herr Braun's cooperage on the riverbank while he rode off on a rented horse to look for Garnet and Stephan.

"Well there you are, you good-for-nothing gill netter!" Heinie Braun yelled when Aaron spoke to him from the door of the shop. "I figured you were going to let me rot in this blasted place all summer."

"We had to get our buildings done at the creek; you knew that. We're a month later than we meant to be in setting our main gangs of nets."

"Well, do you want me or don't you?"

"We want you, and two others like you if we could get them. I have to go down Oconto-way and look for my uncle who's bringing the horses around the bay by land. Gather up a bunk roll and be ready when I come back—and Heinie, I hope we have a rough trip back to the fishery. I want to see what kind of a sailor you are."

"You said last winter there'd be no road to your clearing. How far must a man walk at that place to find a drink and a girl?"

"Two hours going and a night-long stumble coming home if you're drunk or wrung out. But any girl you find in Cedar Forks will be spoken for by the time you get there. Anyway don't you worry, with setting and lifting gill nets from daybreak till noon, gutting and salting fish and making barrels from noon till pitch dark, you won't have the urge."

"You want to bet?"

Aaron had been uneasy about having the husky, hawk-nosed German with the women at the fishery. Besides his careless language, Heinie believed tight pants and a ribald manner were what every woman or girl over the age of fifteen was waiting for. If he ever married a woman, it would not be because he'd wooed her but because he'd overcome her. If he didn't behave at the fishery, they'd have to geld him with hard and continuous work.

Heinie's notions and talk hadn't seemed important during the fighting in the South; a tiger, even an obscene one, was what a man needed for a partner then, but taking him now into a family that was half women was another matter. He was glad he'd not arranged to employ Heinie. Their father had done that.

He crossed the river on a ferry to Marinette, Wisconsin, and walked to Solomon's store where he bought stovepipes to be delivered to the *Flicka* at the cooperage. Later at a livery stable he was offered an impossible choice of a lean brown mare about to foal or a skinny white gelding lamed by a ringbone. He walked back to the stage depot and waited for a ride to Peshtigo, a booming sawmill town several miles down the line. According to the days elapsed, it was probable that he would not catch sight of Stephan and Garnet before he came to Oconto or Pensaukee. It shouldn't be too hard to spot two scrawny old people riding a dun and a black horse.

The stage horses were strong and adequate for their task which was a relief on the frontier where each horse was expected to do the work of two on half rations of oats. He sat on a long board seat beside a rank old lumberjack who still had on the clothes he'd worn to the pine camp in the fall. Facing him was another hard bench where two drummers bounced, ballasted with their cases and carpet bags.

Looking past the drummers' heads and out the open side of the stage, he saw in his mind the magnificent stand of white pine that covered whole townships north beyond his gaze. At that time, in Wisconsin or Michigan, a man who could and would work could have his pick. He could log the great trees, keg the numberless fish in the lakes, farm the virgin soil or mine the veins of copper and iron in the earth.

Except for the Pale Horse and Rider who galloped about scattering typhoid, lung fever and blood poisoning, the north country was the Promised Land. Settlers who escaped this traveler's itinerary marked each day by thanksgiving. But the Johannsen clearing would be visited by this spectre on horseback before the year was up.

Sandy ruts slowed the stage and a cloud of no-see-ums invaded the conveyance. Aaron discarded his morbid thoughts and spoke pleasantly to the salesmen who were slapping the insects and fidgeting with the cases at their feet. Two lids snapped open simultaneously. One case glittered with women's jewelry and the other with watches, fobs and stickpins.

"We sell, you buy, Herr Mister?" both of the men asked, the younger repeating the words of the older.

Aaron saw that they were brothers traveling together for safety. They had the look of having been raised on rutabagas and had not the collective strength to stave off a mildly determined highwayman over the age of twelve.

"I might buy something," he told the men. "It depends on your prices." It would be fun to surprise the womenfolk at home with trinkets such as these.

The older peddler who looked like the Polish Hebrew he'd seen in Copenhagen held out a handful of rings and brooches. "You haf vife, mama? I haf real gold, real gems. See, amethyst, sapphire, opal, garnet, topaz. I make you price."

Aaron picked up a pin with a glowing red, emerald-cut stone and he knew he had to have this namesake jewel for Garnet. "It's getting late in the day," he reminded the salesmen. "Do you plan to stay the night at the hotel on the main street of Peshtigo? I'll pick out three bosom pins and a small ring there. You'll find me by the front window. I'm looking for an elderly aunt and uncle who're traveling north by horseback."

"We hope you meet them soon. You think they buy watch?"

"No."

It was then Aaron realized he'd called a Negro aunt, not auntie.

Waiting his turn at the outhouse before stage time the next morning, Aaron was alerted by one of the vehicles moving in heavy traffic on the street in front. He'd practically had his pants down, but his body tightened up and he sprinted after a wagon loaded with furniture and unmistakably drawn by Kate and Buck. "My God! Somebody's knocked the old couple in the head and stolen my horses!'' he cried to the jewelry drummers as they step- ped aside for him in the path.

As he raced down the sawdust street, his mind was stunned to a standstill by two questions. How could they care for their mother without Garnet? How could he prove that Kate and Buck belonged to him? Though passersby must have thought he was a horse thief himself, he grabbed Buck's bridle and, over a yell of protest by the driver, pulled the team into a sawdust alleyway near the approach to the timber bridge over the Peshtigo River. The horses had been made nervous by the shrieking of the mill saws, and he took them by their bits as he spoke their names.

"Aaron! What are you doing here? Where did you come from?'' A high, surprised voice came from the wagon seat and he saw that the elderly persons driving the load of household goods were Garnet and Stephan. Garnet, wearing Stephan's best Danish suit and cap, sat on the board seat like a wizened teamster's helper.

While Aaron stood there, Stephan, his head cocked and plainly relishing the fact that he'd fooled his grandnephew, grin- ned and went into an explanation. "I had saddle sores before we got to Sturgeon Bay. My hind end is not as tough as Garnet's. I took some money I've had for a long time in my money belt and bought a wagon and harness. We got the furniture and stove in Oconto yesterday. Last night we camped in a graveyard.''

The horses calmed and Aaron walked around to the back of the wagon where a shiny black cookstove was wedged between a walnut bedstead and a matching dresser. Suddenly and for no sen- sible reason he was on the verge of tears for the first time since his visit to Henning's grave in a distant Appalachian churchyard.

Rolling along the sandy ruts to Marinette with Garnet seated between them, he inquired of Stephan about their trip.

"I'd never've made it without my partner here.'' the old man assured him. "She made camp and had the horses harnessed in the morning. She read the map a feller drew for us and always knew which way to go.''

Aaron hugged their child-skinny shoulders to him and withheld praise that would have made them uncomfortable.

"How be Miss Helga?'' Garnet asked when she could do so without butting into the conversation. "We hustle fast, but dat trace around de water be bad.''

"Ma needs you very much,'' Aaron told her. "That's why I was on my way to meet you. I sailed the *Flicka* to Menominee to get Heinie Braun and August Gretuzmacher and came the rest of the way by stage.''

"Helga's worse?'' There was a pitch of anxiety in Stephan's thin, high voice.

"She doesn't say anything. She just walks the floor if she can't sleep, but it's not the same as when Aunt Garnet is there.''

"We thought about that,'' Stephan said.

"The damp cold in her new house aggravates Ma's pain. I bought some pipes so we can set up her cookstove when I get home with the boat. By the way, did you realize you will have to offload your cargo onto the *Guld* when you reach Cedar Forks?''

"We thought of that too.''

Aaron pulled up the horses and handed the lines to his uncle. "You know, you didn't give me a chance to get in the privy back at the hotel,'' he said. "I have to go in the brush right now.''

On the road again, he asked himself, would I have stopped for that purpose if Garnet had been a white woman? The answer shamed and disturbed him and he put the thought away and began to calculate. If the old folks' wagon started up the Bay de Noc Road as soon as it crossed on the ferry to the Michigan side, Stephan and Garnet would be in Cedar Forks on the evening of the morrow. By noon of the third day hence, they'd ride the horses into the fishery clearing as Mandy and Gunnar Nicholson had done two months before.

Mandy certainly was a beautiful Swede girl. Every time her father had taken a stitch in the built-up boot he made for him, Olaf had been there. Olaf said the Nicholson family was coming to spend a Sunday at the fishery as soon as the Johannsens were settled. Now another elemental question arose—the complications of starting a wilderness fishery seemed to be daily compounding. How would they keep Heinie Braun away from a girl as pretty as Mandy?

13

Inherit the Wind

The last half of June, Liza lived in simple terror of the wind, and there was a good reason for her state of mind. For a few days after their arrival from Ephraim, she'd been enchanted by the beach in front of the fishery and had taken Naomi to play there while Aaron strung a new net. Then a fisherman had been lost from a wind-swamped boat and the Johannsen men had begun to talk about some of the numerous sailing accidents on the lakes.

Before long, she'd come to realize that most of these tragedies had been caused by the power and unpredictable nature of the wind. From that time on, fearing the drowned man would wash ashore at her feet, she'd found no pleasure in walking barefoot on the cool, wet sand with Naomi.

Lately, each morning at first light, she'd gone to the small bedroom window to seek out the leafing top branches of an aspen tree at the corner of the garden to ascertain from it the wind's velocity and direction. If the tree swayed gently, the men would have breeze enough to make good sailing time to their nets set two miles from shore, and Mama Johannsen would not haunt her front window with a spyglass.

Today, long before dawn light, Liza had been awakened by the sound of driven surf. She sat up in bed in her high-necked, long-sleeved muslin nightgown. The garment was heavy and hand-woven. She'd borne Norris Peake's child in it and it would survive the births of Aaron's children in this outland beyond roads and doctors. Now, where in the invisible wall on her left hand was the square of mosquito-netted window? Would the waves building on the great body of water at their doorstep spill over the clearing in the pitch-black dark? What was to prevent them? How could a low welt of sand bristled with dune grass contain the wind-shoved breakers?

Not meaning to, she'd awakened Aaron and he complained in a voice groggy for want of sleep, "Liza, will you lay down and let me get some rest?" He pulled her back against him, flung an imprisoning arm over her and went on, "You women only make it harder for us men when you take on about the weather. I don't like the way that wind sounds either, but if it's fit to sail at all, we have to go out and look to our nets. Do you know how long it would take every hand on this place to knit a new gang of nets if we lost one?"

It was a poor time to speak of what had been on her mind for a week, but the menacing sound of the surf was tearing the words from her. "I cain't help it, I never heard such a carrying on of the weather as it does here on this water. I'd rather grub stumps and milk a dozen cows than have to be worried sick about the least storm that comes out of the sky."

He released her and settled back in his depression in the feather bed. "Well I'm no farmer and you knew it. I'm a fisherman and I also worry when the wind doesn't blow. You know we had to dump fifty dollars worth of fish overboard last week when we were becalmed and had to scull ashore. Now go to sleep so you can plant your late potatoes tomorrow. You have plenty of farming to do right here."

His voice drifted off and he was asleep. It was true, if they were ever going to be able to raise their own feed for their animals, there were pole fences to build and enough stump grubbing to make an old man out of a boy. The men had chinked the walls of the three cabins with sphagnum moss, but mortar had to be troweled into the cracks, inside and out.

It had puzzled her from the first that Aaron's people were well-to-do by the day's standards, but able-bodied Johannsen women were expected to do much of the farming work.

She lay still for a moment then slid her bare feet onto the rough boards of the floor, and lifting them to avoid splinters, felt her way into the main room of the cabin. It was as dark as the inside of a closed hearth oven except for the faint blocks of the windows. She faced right, which she knew to be south, and saw with relief that there was no light at all in the direction of Mama Johannsen's house. Aaron's father sometimes panicked when his wife was in pain too hard to bear without walking the floor and went for Garnet who was working much too hard to be up nights.

Turning, she remembered with a start that Heinie Braun was sleeping in their second bedroom. If she roused him, he would come out with his candle and catch her in her nightdress with her hair down. The evening before, when she'd come to the supper table in a clean dress and apron, he'd undressed her with a raised brow and a quizzical eye the color of blued steel. Aaron hadn't seen that, but Heinie's persistent good night wink galled him.

With her fingertips on the log wall, she slipped back into her room and ran a groping hand over Naomi on the cot at the foot of the bed before she crawled in with Aaron. It was good to belong in bed with a kind and ardent man again, to lay peacefully back to back, waiting for him to turn over if he wanted to. At once sorrow for Aaron's parents flowed over her. Though they still shared the same bed, they were separated by a bundling board of infirmity and pain.

She put the thought from her and tried to sleep. Aaron was right, they needed all the rest they could get; but oblivion escaped her as she listened to the wind and pondered the problem of feeding Heinie Braun.

Garnet was lucky, she had August Greutzmacher, a limber-thin, towering angel of a man, in her spare bedroom and at her table. He praised her cooking, but as a mason he was as slow as blackstrap in winter and was plaguing Aaron's father no end.

When the clock, a wedding gift from Olaf, struck four, she rose and dressed by the half-light of a sun still hiding its orb behind the dark hulk of a distant island. The kindling box was full but she went outside to the chopping block at the woodpile for an apron-ful of chips. Firing up the dear and convenient iron cooking stove Mandy Nicholson had freighted up from Menominee was the best chore of her day.

Heinie Braun had been impossible to cook for at best, but he'd claimed the food she'd cooked over an outdoor fire the first days of his sojourn with them had been half raw. Recently he'd been eating more than his share of ham and eggs, Garnet's white bread and Helga's blackberry jam at breakfast time, and Liza had seen the helpless fury in Aaron's eyes.

There'd been so little of Stephan's wedding gift ham left that she'd served it only to the German while she, Naomi and Aaron ate biscuits and milkless porridge sweetened with maple sugar bought from a canoeful of Indians. Maybe the cow, due to freshen any day, would have a heifer and in time they could have breakfast butter and milk the year around.

She'd been uneasy as she'd slighted Aaron on the man food in the mornings. What if Aaron had to fight Heinie? She'd have been feeding up the wrong man. Well today there'd be no favorites. Her household was going to have biscuits, some of the sorghum Garnet had found in a store in Green Bay and fried rainbow trout for breakfast. The ham and jam were gone.

At the house door, she stood on the doorstep with her load of chips and shivered in the cold, water-chilled air. If the wind laid entirely, the tender plants in the garden would be black by another morning. She felt half a world away from Tennessee and homesick for the first time at the fishery.

When the cooking fire was burning good, she covered the rough plank table with the only tablecloth she'd saved from the war. Heinie Braun wasn't worth the trouble, but Aaron was. He wanted very much to board Heinie as well as Mrs. Braun had boarded him when he was the Brauns' apprentice. Somehow in a spare and alien land, the German lady managed to acquire meats and cheeses and even fruits for pastries.

Aaron dressed and came to the kitchen door when the smell of browning fish filled the house, then he stepped around to the other bedroom to beg Heinie to get up.

Liza drew the coffee pot to the back of the stove to settle the brew, opened the oven door to let the burning heat off the high, brown, soda-and-cream-of-tartar biscuits and turned the pieces of trout skin-side-up to keep them hot. With everything ready to be put on the table, she went to Aaron where he stood at the washing and shaving shelf on the wall near the outside door, smoothing his red, cowlicked hair as he combed it. It was almost full light now. With one arm squeezing her waist, he grinned at her and said, "Mrs. Johannsen, you do look pretty this morning—if we were alone, we could go back to bed."

"But we're not," she whispered. Heinie had come into the room and had gone directly to the table without washing. She hurried to put the warm food before their guest and poured the coffee while Aaron seated himself on a wall bench behind the table.

She sat down and had barely raised her head from saying a silent grace when Naomi called, "Ma? I can't button my back."

As she started in to her daughter, Aaron was saying pleasantly to Heinie, "Did you hear that wind a couple of hours ago? I guess you're going to get some experience in tacking with the boat today."

The German took two slabs of fish and two biscuits on his

plate then gave it a disgusted shove. Naomi began to talk as she entered the bedroom, but Liza could hear Heinie say in the kitchen, "Well now, Aaron, when are you going to teach that mountain woman how to cook some good Deutsch food?"

Aaron's tone was cold and his breakfast would be the same in his stomach. "She'll cook it when she gets it."

Heinie had retrieved his plate for he was speaking with food in his mouth. "Don't be so touchy. I just got a belly full of wormy hardtack and rancid pork sides during the war," he was half apologizing.

"I know," Aaron agreed, but Liza knew he was spoiling to hew Heinie down to size.

Sitting on the bed, combing Naomi's long dark hair, she had no need of her gift of second sight to see that the Johannsen fishery, wedged between the boundless forest and the bounding bay, was going to be battle-scarred ground before the year was up.

More than that, whatever skirmishes took place here, Aaron's father would be at the center. He'd influenced his family to take on more than they could do and now, torn by his wife's illness, he was cantankerous beyond bearing. One day Aaron would confront his own father if the older man did not stop being so perverse with their mother. Papa Johannsen was beside himself; he wouldn't let Mama Johnnsen be sick and he wouldn't let her be well.

In late April, much against their inclinations, the boys had hauled two boat loads of hen and cow manure from Ephraim to the new landing. Without fertilizer, their flowers, garden vegetables and potatoes wouldn't have grown worth anything in the secondary beach of the old Indian corn plot. Then on a Sunday early in May, a month before the cabins were ready, Aaron had sailed her, Garnet and Stephan from Ephraim with a boat load of carefully dug and packed peonies and hardy plants from Helga's peninsula garden. Leander had discouraged them from that labor of love. "Those plants won't bloom this year, anyway," he argued.

But the flowers had been planted and were thriving. The heartsease had not been set back at all and one of Helga's cherished double white "pineys" had two full blooms out of a dozen stalks. No matter how badly Aaron's mother felt, she went out and looked at them the first thing in the morning and the last thing at night. Now Helga's flower garden, an area enclosed by the long side of the house and a discarded gill net fence, was a sight to see, the only spot in Michigan that reminded Liza of her homeland.

After breakfast, Liza kept her eyes away from the open door as she tidied the house and attempted once more to mix a batch of white bread as good as Garnet's. Unlike Mama Johannsen, she felt easier when she refrained from monitoring the progress of the boats out on the lake, whether it was as windy as it was today or not. It was like a man going off to war; if it was God's will that he come home, he'd come home. Not until the Johannsens began to furl the sails of their heavily laden craft as they came ashore, was she daily relieved of the anxiety that washed at her.

Later as she left her house with Naomi to go to the potato field, she saw that Helga, wearing the type of sunbonnet she'd adopted from the Tennessee women, was already in her garden with the dog Tippy. Naomi ran across their own bare yard and entered the oasis of her step-grandmother. "Grandma Johannsen, cain I stay and help you a while?" she inquired. "I'll drop taters for Ma when she gets the holes dug."

"Indeed you can," Helga promised and waved a stem of spicy pink dianthus under Naomi's nose. "We'll go down to the bay and get some water for this lovely container that makes the magic elixir that puts the green in the leaves and the color in the flowers."

Liza looked past Helga's "manure tea" barrel, standing in a corner of the garden and raised on stones so a bucket could be set under the dripping bung hole. To the south, Garnet and Stephan were on the sloping roof of the cooperage, nailing shingles. The old couple were as sweetly matched as mortises in a cupboard door. In spite of Aaron's father's skepticism, they didn't have to be able to make love. They were love.

Helga and Naomi went chattering off to the bay for a bucket of water and Liza started off to the piece of rough-plowed ground at the edge of the cabin pole slashing with a bag of seed potatoes, a hoe and a ball of twine. She was walking slowly along the end of the vegetable garden, pleased by the sign of greening rows, when she heard an angry shout.

Leander was stomping over the small bridge from the net shed where he'd been working. He met his wife as she came to the back of her fertilizer barrel which she filled from outside the net fence. "I told you before, Helga, "he shouted loudly. "I will not stand for you to lug water for some no good flowers. You'll bust something inside."

Liza wavered in the path, debating whether she should go back and get Naomi, when Helga and the little girl made sounds like screams clapped behind hands. She dropped her burdens and reversed her direction, reluctant to intervene, but pressed to be near her child if Leander was out of control.

Helga had partly screened the offensive cask from within the garden with tubbed oleander and flowering maple house plants. As she hurried back now, Liza could see Helga and Naomi inside the fence, standing at the edge of a spreading, odorous mess. The oleander was snapped off, smashed by the overturned barrel, the white-white of the peony was crushed and inundated, and evil-smelling flotsam was overflowing the pointed buds of a creeping rose moss bed.

Leander had given the weighty barrel a hard push or kick in a moment of blind anger. Now he seemed to be in shock, repeating, "I told you I would put an end to this foolishness. I told you."

In the garden with Naomi squatting beside her, Liza raked away the ooze from the succulent-leaved portulaca with her finger tips. Helga was running with the dog to the beach. Leander stumbled through the gate and walked in a daze between the resented flower beds. He stood directly behind Naomi, blowing his nose and making distracted scratchings in the sand with his boot toe. Was he out of his mind? Would he kick one of them in the head? Liza pulled Naomi around on her far side and waited for a blow or a word. She fought down an impulse to stand up and fling a handful of the stinking soup in his face.

Finally the man behind her was able to say, "I'll go and plant potatoes if you clean up Helga's flowers for her and make her feel better."

Liza stood up with Naomi, and before she could stop her, the child accused, "Grandpa Johannsen, ye be a bad man."

"Aye, I be."

Liza looked away from a man full of miseries and was thankful that Naomi's outburst had saved her from making a retort she'd be sorry for. "Who else will mend your fences?" she asked after a moment of thought. "The black woman on your shed roof? Don't you think you'd better go and make your wife feel better yourself?"

"Aye, I'll go. I'll do what you say."

He went toward the bay and the wind flapped his shirt away from this thinning body. He cut across a dune between two prostrate junipers and intercepted his wife as she approached the cedars on the sandy point.

Liza held her filthy hands from her and Naomi plucked at her sleeve. "Will Grandpa Johannsen make Grandma Johannsen cry?"

No, the couple stood as one figure now on the lonely beach. Presently they walked on, and the small dog ran ahead, flushing screaming herring gulls into white-winged flight.

14

Nor Things Present Nor Things to Come

Horrified and breathless, Leander saw that Helga meant to elude him by running into the breaking sea. His calamitous tantrum at the garden had driven her as disappointment, pain and the prospect of agony had not been able to do.

Seizing her, he held her by the arm, too roughly he knew, but she was struggling with unexpected strength. Tippy leaped at them and almost downed them in their twofold misery. He fended the animal off with his foot and led Helga up the beach. Her face was obscured by the brim of her mountain-style head covering, and he was glad of that for the moment—only hurt, loathing or anger could be hidden there.

The dog left them to chase a bird scurrying through the reeds. They walked on; he felt the tenseness leave her, and her hand was warm in his. He must speak quickly, apologize somehow, though there was no easy way to say he was abjectly sorry for what had happened. "Now I've done it," he began. "I know what I did is too bad for you to forget. All I can say is, my life is worth nothing anymore. Not to me, to no one. But I live for you. I even lost my temper for you."

They had rounded the point now and Helga, faltering and gasping from emotion and exertion, dropped onto a chair-high boulder. The wind billowed the slatted visor of her bonnet as she looked up at him. Was the expression on her face contempt or indifference? When she'd caught her breath, she said flatly, "Leander, you're a liar." Her usually mobile face was an enigma, and he was terrified. In thirty years she'd not spoken to him so.

"You're twice a liar," she continued. Her eyes were fixed far out in the full-swelling bay where the boys were, and he profoundly longed to be with them there.

"I don't know what you mean."

"You make a lie out of the fact that I'll not be here on this beach with you another summer, but worst of all you say your only concern is for me."

"It is for you! I will not live without you."

"See, Leander? You've said it yourself. Think of what you said."

"I have no one else but you, no one else would put up with me. Little Naomi said I am a bad man and I am."

Before she could reply, he realized where she was sitting and jumped up from his crouching position at her feet, pulling her up with him. "You must not sit on cold stone!" he cried. "That is no good for you."

He picked her up and carried her a few rods from the water to the prone bole of a long dead tree in a sunny spot among the ground-sweeping cedars. Here they must say what they'd been unable to express in quiet times over a cup of coffee or in bed. He waited, hoping she would initiate this inevitable discussion, but she was silent now, withdrawn, gazing at the rhythmic crests on the horizon. A schooner wallowed toward the lower end of the bay; but the boys' boats, sails furled at the nets, were hidden by the heaving water.

Finally she said, "You know we must come to an understanding about things. We can't have more of what happened today."

"You tell me what I must do. For months I have not been able to think, only about how sick you will be. I've begged God for a miracle so you can be with me."

Sitting beside him, she caressed his hand then and held it against her thin but warm and living cheek. "You must grow old sweetly in the bosom of our beautiful family. You must start letting me go by allowing me to be your wife again as long as I am able. You must stop thinking of yourself."

"How can you ask me to do such things? Who will help me when you're not here? I will be dead then, but they will not bury me."

"Leander?"

If Helga had ever needed anything, it was a strong and brave man now, a man who could refrain from flinging his body over her lap and sobbing like a brokenhearted child. She settled against him, and he put both arms around her as he had in the park in Copenhagen when they were courting.

She went on determinedly, "Leander, untie the knots in your jaws, loose your heart and stomach so we can talk. Maybe we'll never be in this mood again."

"I'll try, we'll talk."

"I think I'll begin by telling you about something Garnet read to me last night—I remember this much, 'For I am persuaded, that neither death nor life...nor things present nor things to come, nor height nor depth...shall separate us from the love of God, which is in Christ Jesus our Lord.' Leander, if we trust God and each other, He will never truly separate *us*."

"But Helga, how can God take the breath out of my body and leave my flesh. I will be a walking dead man, a zombie like Garnet told you about."

"You'll work and be a loving grandfather. When this is over, you'll be Captain Johannsen again. You'll do something every day that I'd have done. I'll depend on you for that. You'll endure, and when you're old, you'll come to me and we'll run hand in hand, whole and strong, as we did before we were married."

He took away his arms, touched her hand briefly in her lap, then rising blindly, stumbled from her and crashed through a deadfall behind them to the trunk of a virgin hemlock. He pressed himself into the rough bark of the tree to still the spasms of grief that threatened to disassemble his body. But the sound of his weeping was covered by the noise of the sea and the soughing of the heavy branches above him. His strength seeped away and he slumped to the ground.

The terrier found him there and frantically licked the tears from his face. He embraced the animal, which was not his habit; and shaking off the remnant of daze, he went to Helga where she sat in the wind on a piece of driftwood near the water.

Her eyes were not on the lake but were lifted to the top of the tree where he'd been. Glancing back, he heard and saw the brown thrasher in the topmost branches. The restless, rufous bird trilled and sang a medley of hymns, but no exultations were repeated.

"See how God speaks to us," Helga said, adding, "do you believe in signs, Leander?"

"Aye, I do. I hear everything that bird says."

"And what's he telling you?" Her face was breaking into a smile.

"Go home and clean up the mess you made."

Helga laughed as she had not in months. She hugged him and tugged him homeward. "Indeed you must; when we've had some coffee and some rest, I'll help you. Remember? The Nicholsons are coming on Sunday."

The scolding gulls took back their vantage point and the brown thrasher flew to a coppice of willow brush where his mate had her nest.

15

Undertow

"Don't belittle your legs," Aaron told Liza. "They're the reason I married you. Our Johannsen men were getting shorter all the time and we needed some long-legged blood." They'd been lying in bed, talking on a Sabbath morning alive with birdsong.

Liza got up and he watched as she sat on the edge of the bed, loosening her dark braids for the morning brushing. It was a deal of trouble, keeping heavy, knee-length hair smelling freshly washed in hot weather. It had taken Garnet several hours the afternoon before to shampoo his mother's and Liza's hair in warm brook water and towel the tresses dry in the sun on the dock.

He reached for his wife's arm, questioning, "What're you so solemn about all of a sudden?"

"I'm thinking that Papa Johannsen's looking for us to have a youngun ahead of time and it may be he won't be far wrong."

"Well now, don't you worry," he reassured her. "If you give Pa his first grandson, he'll forget he knows how to count even if you do fall down and bring on the baby before he's expected."

Aaron knew Liza was superstitious about being drawn into a conversation about the sex of an unborn child. "It's a pretty Sunday," she commented, "a fine day for your mama to have Olaf's girl and her family here for dinner."

He went along with his wife's change of subject. "Sundays are always special for Ma, but Pa'd have worked us seven days a week those first years. He's changed some now, but there were times when you could tell he was vexed when she took us to church in the morning and played with us in the afternoon on Sundays.

She skated and rode the sail sled with us in winter and took us for long walks in the woods in summer.''

Abruptly he threw back the quilt and swung his feet to sit beside her. "You know what? I don't think Heinie came home in the night. I bet he figured to ride from the Forks in the *Flicka* when Olaf brings the Nicholsons. Bjorn's been talking too much about how pretty Mandy is.''

Liza stood up and stretched with the pliant grace that had pleased him from the start. "Why don't you look in his room?'' she suggested. "If he's not here, we could let Naomi sleep and we could water your mama's flowers. The water runs out of that sand as fast as it's poured on. There isn't much showing of the damage Papa Johannsen did the first of the week and it's a blessing.''

Standing up to put his pants on, he realized she was seeing him in his linen drawers for the first time in broad daylight. That meant they were old married folks now. He gave his belt a jaunty jerk, but Liza was embarrassed and looked quickly away and out the window where long, low combers rolled in, promising good sailing for Olaf. It would be one of the nicest days they'd have in this climate, but he shivered, not a quivering of muscles but a rippling of intuition.

Liza was dressing almost entirely under her tent-like nightgown though she usually stepped behind the hanging sheet that separated their bed from Naomi's. Modesty abetted mystery and mystery, romantic feelings—but Heinie would have done away with all this hide-and-seek right at the start.

Aaron stepped around the corner into Heinie's room. It was empty. The tall German would be on the *Flicka* all right. He would discomfit Olaf with sly, shady remarks in front of Mandy and her folks. Olaf's new built-up shoe was serving him well, but it would take more than a boot to put him on equal footing with Heinie.

Back in their bedroom again, Aaron said to Liza, "Heinie's not here. Why don't you come in the kitchen and put up your hair while I make a fire in the stove and boil us some coffee? She came with him and stood with hairbrush in hand at the window facing his parents' home. Without her work apron, the yellow dress fitted her long, lissom figure as it had the first night he'd had supper with her in Tennessee. But not for long—all would be changed, come winter.

"I saw a light at your mama's agin last night,'' she said.

"I didn't get up and look. I was so relieved when I saw Aunt

Garnet and Uncle Stephan lugging their feather bed to Ma's house last evening.''

"I was too, but we'll have to spell the old folks all we can. The extry menfolk can eat here so Garnet can rest when your mama does.''

"I'll tell Pa today so he understands.''

He went to her and held her slim body, and the unbraided half of her hair circled his shoulder and enclosed them in a silky cocoon. "Liza," on impulse he decided to say outright what had been on his mind since April. "Liza, maybe I'll be too bashful or taken up with trouble to tell you this again—I want you to know I realize the Johannsens would have been in a fix without you and Garnet. With Annie so far away, tending Ma and doing the work of three women would have been a hard business for us men.''

"I reckon God knowed that.''

"He made a true believer out of me by sending you Tennessee women.''

She loosed herself from him and sat on Heinie's chair. "Olaf was saying one day that Mandy's daddy has a Bible from the old country. People come to his setting room of a Sabbath and he reads and talks to them in Swedish.''

"Good. Liza! do you know what you just said?''

"No.''

"We could ask Carl Nicholson to do the same for Ma when he comes. She has a Swedish Bible.''

"I reckon that'd pleasure her the most of ary thing I know.''

"It hit me that things had taken a turn for the worse when Garnet and Stephan sent Olaf and Bjorn off to their cabin to sleep and moved in with Ma and Pa. I thought then, I've been thinking for weeks, of how Ma misses the little church in Ephraim. I've tried to figure out how we could take her back there once more, but the trip'd be too hard for her.''

"That chapel meant more to her than ary spot on earth. It's too bad there be none of such hereabouts.''

"There will be someday, but not in time for Ma.''

Liza wound and pinned her braided hair and he stood at the table, mixing pancakes to stay them until the bountiful meal the women were planning for noonday. Though this was the scarcest time of year for provisions, their mother had found foods for a feast.

Liza began to set the table, but her eyes reflected a preoc- cupied mind. Finally she spoke and at first her proposal was incomprehensible, "We can't have a brush arbor messing up the beach. There's no time and your daddy'd not stand for it nohow. But we could carry the organ out on the dock, there's hardly no mosquitoes there. We could have a real meeting to surprise your mama."

He laid his hand on her arm in a praising gesture. "Why not? You just tell me what to do."

"It's only six o'clock. Soon's we eat, you could help Uncle Stephan with his chores while I bake the dried peach pies. Then I'll talk to Garnet and we'll water the flowers when Naomi gets up."

"She's up now." Naomi had come, half asleep, from the bedroom in her nightgown. The little girl leaned against him and he held her to his thigh with his free hand while he turned hotcakes with the other.

It was queer seeming, but the tougher the circumstances of life, the more partial he became to women. There'd be no use at all, fighting the bay and the wind and cold, without gentle, caring womenfolk ashore. It struck him then, the nature of his father's anguish.

The crude sawhorse table on the *Flicka's* dock was his mother's and Liza's inspired idea for a family dinner. A light current of water-cooled air flowed up the brook and pushed the heat of the July sun from the site.

"I'll get a tarp and cover these odds and ends of lumber," Aaron told August Greutzmacher who'd helped him assemble the make-shift picnic board. "Maybe you could see how many benches they can spare from the houses and bring them here."

"When we're done, I'll just sit a while and look," the thin but wide-shouldered mason responded and his serene glance swept the lake and forest boundaries of the settlement. "In such a place I would have had my family."

Aaron knew August's wife and two young sons had died on the Atlantic on a plague-scourged emigrant ship twenty years before. August had asked one day, "This water goes somehow to the ocean?" It was clear that living at the edge of the broad expanse of Green Bay had brought the middle-aged man more peace than he'd known in all his wanderings.

With a table and seating contrived, Aaron sat a few minutes to visit with the stonecutter. "Life would be good here on the Michigan shore if Ma's trouble and too much work doesn't get the best of us," he said meditatively. "Except for Heinie, we've all been overdrawing our strength."

"Men and women do that in a new land," August reflected.

"I guess it's that or live like animals."

"If your mama was well, the worst would be over. A man has to work and die and be buried someplace. I think this is one of the best."

"You'd stay here?"

"I would and I'd be grateful for the chance."

"For your keep in your old age, would you be a friend to Pa when he's left alone?"

"Aaron, I would. I sure would. And I'll dress staves and work on the buildings as long as I can."

How different August was from Heinie, though Mrs. Braun and August were brother and sister. Aaron clasped the huge, hard stoneworker's hand of the older man where it lay at rest on the canvas covered table. "I'll speak to Uncle Stephan and Pa, just to make sure, but I don't think you need to worry. You've found a place where you'll be part of a family."

"I might get sick before my work is done."

"I guess people are always half ailing these days. Like the Indians, we have to accept that as a fact of life."

August nodded. "Someday that will not be so. We won't have to be afraid of a new sickness every time a boatload of settlers comes in."

Their father had watered the flowers before anyone else had gotten to it and now he was walking slowly with their mother in the vegetable plot behind the house. August left the table and walked back to his room in Garnet's cottage. Naomi came and sat beside him on the bench, smoothing her pink dimity skirt with careful brown hands. His mother had made the matching bonnet and dress on the new sewing machine. They'd teased her about learning a new trade and she'd answered, "It may be my first, last and only time, but it was fun."

It was a good day. In their pens the cows and horses, pigs and chickens were eating hay and grain brought ashore in June from a schooner anchored out in the bay. The feed had been conveyed to the dock in a scow with the aid of the team, a cable and a ground anchor set in sufficiently deep water. Except in winter when dray teams traveled on the ice, all the kegged fish would be loaded on freighters by the same laborious method.

A many-colored Mediterranean hen coaxed a rainbow of

chicks over the plank bridge on her way to the garden where she'd look up and down the rows for insects for her brood. Naomi jumped down to follow them at a prudent distance, hoping to catch a fluffy laggard.

Helga and Leander made their way back to the dock, and Aaron forced himself to return his mother's stark smile. God! she was only a wraith of the woman she had been. His father went to the house to fetch a jacket for her, and she spoke as animatedly as ever, "You know, Aaron, this truly is the day the Lord hath made. I asked Garnet to give me only a little medicine so I could enjoy it."

"I'm waiting for all the good food you're going to have on this table at dinnertime." He patted his stomach, indicating hunger, then added, "Wait. Did you hear something?"

The *Flicka* would come silently except for waterborne voices, but this had been a glad hail from ashore, up the beach path to the Forks. The Nicholsons' bay horses, Gert and Sam, came around the point walking energetically. What had happened to the *Flicka*? Then he saw the horses' riders. "Ma! Ma, look!" he cried. "You were right! This *is* the day!"

She sprang from the bench and ran off the dock to meet his father. "Leander! Leander, Anna's here!"

Naomi darted back to the picnic table and picked at his sleeve. "Who be those folks, Uncle Aaron?"

"They're your Aunt Annie, Uncle Walter and baby Maggie."

"Helga, wait!" his father called in panic, but she was already hanging, swaying and gasping, on Gert's mane when they reached the travelers.

Walter Langenberg had slipped from Sam's bare back and was helping ten-month-old Maggie and her mother down from Gert. Annie let her husband take the baby and held her own mother, comforting her, "Don't cry, Mama. Olaf wrote us to come and surprise you, and we came."

But her angry flag-blue eyes met his and Aaron read their message with dismay: Aaron, oh, Aaron, how could you? Why didn't you let us know Ma was so sick?

He'd forgotten how tiny Annie and Walter were. Annie had married Walter as much for his happy-go-lucky disposition as anything; yet a man so slighted in stature would have to have something working for him besides amiability and blond good looks. Walter's manhood had never been in question. Though he and Annie had bodies like adolescents, they had produced one robust baby and were plainly trying for another.

"We came up from Menominee on the Bay de Noc stage," Walter told them when he could get a word in edgewise. "What a ride! We stayed at the Nicholsons last night and left there about seven this morning. Annie didn't want to ride in the boat."

"No, I didn't!" Annie laughed now. "I took one look at Gert and I knew she'd be the best transportation for Maggie and me. She's been a mother herself, she carried us like a basket of eggs."

Aaron helped their father lift their mother to a sidesaddle seat on Gert's blanketed back. Then Naomi spoke to him through an insistent jerk on his trouser leg and he set her on Sam.

"Look, Naomi," his mother told the child, "I'm Queen Victoria and you're my lady-in-waiting."

Annie, holding the skirt of her high-waisted brown dress aside for walking, cried, "Oh, Ma! You are."

Annie's vivid ways called up a colorful picture of their mother as Aaron first remembered her and his head whirled counterclockwise to his stomach. He held on to Sam's bridle for help in propelling his devitalized legs.

Liza and Stephan were standing on the dock, and the white terrier came barking and splashing from under it. Annie stooped, and Tippy threw his wet body into lovingly remembered arms, was hugged then put down. Even with pregnancy distorting her center of gravity, Annie ran forward with easy agility to take Liza's hands. "Oh you are just as pretty and slim as Uncle Stephan said," she cried. "I just curled up with joy when I heard how you and Aaron found each other."

Stephan and Garnet had spent the night at the Langenbergs' home when they traveled through the Green Bay area with the horses. "Uncle Stephan, Where's your Garnet?" Annie wanted to know.

"*Fader var är i himmelen*," (Our Father which art in heaven,) Carl Nicholson's resonant voice belied the fragility of the body he'd propped upright on two crutches. "*Helgadt varde dit name.*" (Hallowed be thy name.)

Helgadt. Aaron wondered if their mother's name, Helga, meant hallowed. He knew the name had been chosen in Finland for the middle of nine babies born to the Swedish Aaronsons of Vasa, but her parents could have hardly known how dearly appropriate the name might seem to her son half a century later.

Some of the eighteen people at the picnic table on the dock followed the Lord's Prayer in High German, Plattdeutsch, Norwegian and American mountain English, but Aaron separated his mother's and the Nicholsons' Swedish from the rest.

Earlier, Liza had hovered near Aaron when the Nicholsons had arrived in the *Flicka*, wordlessly prodding him and Aaron had asked their guest, "Mr. Nicholson, can you read Swedish?"

"Aye."

"We wanted to ask you if you'd read a few words out of Ma's Bible before we eat. She is lonesome for our little church in Ephraim."

"Aye, that I would. Olaf mentioned about his mother in the boat. He says you haf an organ und a lady who can play it. She haf hymnbook?"

"Yes."

A brief service had been hastily planned at Helga's bedside where she was resting, and now they all sat at the linen-covered table, set for a rustic banquet except for the food.

Aaron glanced sideways at his mother. Serenity had smoothed and filled her countenance and there was a transference, through hands held under the tablecloth, to their father's face. How beautiful she was! The words had almost been articulated aloud from the depths of him. At the end of the table he saw the furrowed faces of Stephan and Carl Nicholson and thought: I'll be older than they are before I forget this day. I'll remember still when my sons and Annie's are grandfathers. God bless Olaf for writing to Annie. He looked at Mandy Nicholson, fetchingly garbed in a thin blue summer dress and a lace-edged scoop bonnet. Would she ever suspect the depth and goodness of his brother?

Garnet sat at the organ the men had easily carried from the house. Stephan had dropped his hands between his knees and Aaron could see the tendons straining, though the old man had heard his companion play daily and well.

Tall and firm-figured, Dorcas Nicholson got up now and stood by Garnet's side, facing the table. Born at almost the same time and place as their mother, she too had the sapphire-blue eyes and dark hair of many Finlander-Swede women.

Garnet had been pumping the organ, now she tentatively touched a key, and at that moment Dorcas Nicholson began to sing, "We gather together to ask the Lord's blessing. He chastens and hastens His will to make known."

Watching their mother's face, Aaron knew that Dorcas Nicholson's full and bell-timbred voice was the best of all gifts for the day.

How did the soaring notes affect the rest around the table? Stephan had relaxed, but Heinie was poised, barely touching the bench, ready to flee such woman foolishness. August Greutzmacher's face was more tranquil than Aaron had seen it and he had an unconsciously restraining hand on his nephew's arm.

Carl Nicholson had taken up their mother's Bible and was saying, "Now I vant to read to you from St. John, 14. My vife vill tell you in English."

Oh, God, that's the "Let not your heart be troubled" one, Aaron thought. How could Ma have asked for that passage? It can only make this occasion a funeral before time. No, the shoemaker was reading the "vine" verses.

When Carl Nicholson had placed the Bible back on the organ, Liza rose and took their mother by the arm and they went to stand with Mandy, Annie and Dorcas behind Garnet where they all could see the one precious hymnbook from Tennessee. There'd been talk during the War about the Swedish Nightingale, Jenny Lind, but surely mortals had never heard sweeter voices than those blending with the powerful contralto of Dorcas Nicholson, singing the "Crusaders' Hymn."

Were the great pines on the ridge behind the cabin pole slashings swaying to the music? Aaron looked again at Heinie. Perhaps no one else had noticed it, but the proud face was more relaxed now than he had ever known it. The knotted jaw muscles had loosened and Heinie's windburned face was shaped now like the paler, glowing visage of his uncle August.

The women's voices drifted off over the clearing, and Carl Nicholson handed the worn leather Bible to their smiling mother and said, "Vell now, Mrs. Johannsen, I guess ve vill sing, 'Now T'ank ve all our God', und let t'ese boys eat before t'ey starve."

The service was over and Aaron knew by his mother's face that it had been as a memorial should indeed be—before time. After a barely respectful interval of comment and reflection, the women rushed to the houses for pickled salt herring, Stephan's treasured new potatoes, Dorcas Nicholson's new peas, Garnet's brown beans and biscuits, Annie's Belgian cheese and Liza's pies, all to be served with Stephan's egg coffee.

"Annie, you should have got yourself in a family way by a

man big enough to carry you across that crick,'' Walter said. Was
he making a statement of fact or indulging in the tender teasing
that irked his father-in-law?

"Walter, you should know by now, the biggest men have the
smallest families,'' Annie retorted.

It's a good thing Annie doesn't talk that way in front of Ma,''
Aaron said, testing Liza to see if she had been shocked.

"It's her way and no harm to it,'' Liza replied.

Olaf and Mandy, Walter and Annie, Gunnar and Bjorn and
Liza and he were straggling out a skidding trail to the white pine
ridge two hours after the Sunday dinner. Aaron had promised the
girls they could find colonies of tall pink lady's-slipper at the south
base of the pine grove knoll. Heinie had been asked to go along,
but he'd instinctively known he was not truly wanted.

"No. I'll take Uncle August and the skiff and go out hook-
and-line fishing for lake perch,'' he said.

In the woods, everyone except Annie had leaped the four-
foot-wide tributary of the main brook with dry feet. She made as if
to jump a time or two then cocked her head and declared, "If this
ditch was deep enough, I could float across, but it's not so I'll
wade.''

"I'll come back and get you,'' Aaron told her. He was taller
and heavier than her young Hollander husband by three inches
and thirty pounds. "It's all right, Walter,'' he sought to convince
his brother-in-law.

"No, you won't,'' was Annie's reply to that. She'd already
dropped to the ground, slipped off her shoes and having yanked
her skirts above her knees, was untying her stockings. She stood
up, gathered her footwear and her skirts and walked, shrieking,
through the spring-cold water.

Bjorn and Gunnar were snickering over the spectacle and
Bjorn admonished his sister in mock horror, "Annie! You'll have
a web-footed baby.''

"That's all right, we've got a duck pond to raise him in.''
Walter said as he sat on the ground in front of his wife and began
to dry and dress her feet.

How was Olaf taking all this earthy levity? It was hard to
tell—he was kissing Mandy in a way that could only mean one of
two things, a broken heart or an early wedding.

With Annie on her feet again, Aaron led the way up a short,
steep slope that had been the ancient bank of the lake. The hump
of sand that had been ecologically perfect for twenty or thirty

giant white pines was only a few rods wide. The hikers scattered and walked in pairs through the cool redolence, admiring four and five feet thick monarchs rising fifty feet to the first limb.

"I've never seen the beat of such trees." Liza was awestruck. "Be there more?"

Aaron looked up through the sun-glinted arches of a natural nave. "There's thousands of square miles of trees like these in northern Wisconsin and Michigan," he told her and Walter and Annie who'd stopped to listen.

"You won't cut these if they be all you've got, will you?" Liza asked, running her hand down the grooved bark.

"He will," Walter said. "They all do. My father says there'll not be a single white pine like one of these standing when I'm an old man."

"These'll go for barrel staves," Aaron was forced to admit. "They're the reason I bought the land."

Walter lowered himself to a pine-needle-padded chair formed by two buttressing roots and Annie fell into his lap, resting in his arms. She looked up at Liza with a grin. "It's so nice and cool here and I'm too pooped to move another inch. I'll just sit here and let Walter rub my back. The rest of you go ahead and look for flowers with Aaron."

"I told you back at your mama's that this kind of walk would be too much for you," Walter said, soberly this time.

"Pshaw," Annie scoffed, "I'm just gathering strength to race you back to the house. I don't know why I ever let you put my shoes back on my feet. I'll just have to take them off again."

"Hold on!" Aaron stood nearby with his arm around Liza's waist. "We won't cross that river on the way home, there'll be nothing you can't step over free and dry."

"*Aaron! Mr. Aaron, Mr. Aaron!*" Before he located the slight, wheezing figure in the blue kerchief, strength ran from Aaron's pores like water from the sand in his mother's garden. Garnet could run like a deer and she had. The chalk-blue pallor of her face foretold collapse and he jumped forward to keep the old lady from sagging to the ground. "Hush," he said, holding her. "Get your breath. Take your time." He had the despairing notion that if she spoke no more, the blue and white tranquility of the day would be restored.

"Oh, Mr. Aaron..."

"Hush," he repeated.

But Liza, cupping Garnet's stricken face, said urgently, "You must tell us. Who be it?"

"De boat. Mr. August and Heinie done upset de leetle boat. Dey be a body hangin' to hit."

Not their mother! Now that Liza upheld Garnet, Aaron leaned against a tree trunk for support, catching breath enough to speak and run. "Heinie's still with the skiff?" he asked the trembling brown woman.

"Yore mama doan know. She got up and tuk her spyglass like she allus do. Dey be only one man a'clingin'."

His mind had cleared and it snapped into action with the precision of oiled steel. "Bjorn!" he yelled. Then when his brother answered from the ridge, "Come! Run! Heine's had an accident with the boat."

The boys came at once and he flung directives at them, "Gunnar, find Olaf and Mandy and bring the women home." "Bjorn, you come with me."

As he embraced Liza and Garnet and sprang off for the clearing, his mind, clear as a bell now, divided right down the middle. One half watched and drove his feet through the tangled underbrush and over obstacles; he was running faster than man had ever moved over that terrain, and Bjorn was at his heels. The remainder of his brain flashed ahead to the fishery and the catastrophe on the bay. How far out to sea was the skiff? Had Heinie rowed up or down shore? God, let it be up shore for the springing breeze, almost always from the southwest in summer, was veering to the north.

A dozen more airborne bounds and he was in the clearing where in panic he rescinded his appeal of a moment before. Their father and Stephan would be out in the *Flicka*, attempting a rescue. The wind was gusting strongly. If the older men gave the fickle craft too much sail, there'd be a double tragedy like the one off Washington Island a few years before the war. The wispy tops of the limber, bypassed trees in the cutting were bending to the southeast.

Bjorn came alongside him, and he hauled the boy down long enough to instruct him in gasps, "Get the grappling hook...and the long rope...from the net shed."

The *Flicka* was gone as he'd expected, but the stable, flat bottomed *Guld* was in her berth. He reached the dock and steadied himself against the *Flicka's* mooring post, sucking in air to restore vigor to his trembling legs. His mother and the Nicholsons were there, huddled and white, holding Naomi and Maggie at the picnic table. He reached for his mother's telescope and focused on the cause for her obvious terror. The *Flicka* was running full sail before the breeze, a third of her keel out of the water. You could upend a Stahl built boat with too much sail.

Ahead of the scudding *Flicka*, a sandy-haired figure clung to the overturned skiff. There was nothing else in the water. August must have stood up to pull in a fish and capsized the small green boat. *His father and Stephan were going too fast!* They were going to ram the hull to which Heinie clung for his life! *Heinie couldn't swim.*

In the second it took to hand the glass back to his mother, Aaron remembered what August had said that morning when they'd sat in the sun at the completed picnic table. "This is as good a place as any." Now it had happened, and the gentle, sad-faced artisan had been in the water too long for any hope of lifesaving procedures.

His mother held to his arm with desperate strength. "Aaron, please promise me you won't do anything foolish."

"No, Ma." But she knew he'd do what he had to.

Bjorn raced across the bridge with the equipment and they ran to the *Guld*. Carl Nicholson rose to his crutches in an involuntary helping gesture, then he sat down again; but their mother followed them. She stood with one arm around the *Guld*'s mooring post, bracing herself. "Get aboard, I'll untie the boat for you." As sick as she was, she'd do whatever had to be done when the boats were ashore again. She'd comfort Heinie and arrange a funeral for August. She'd be—God willing, for another day, she'd *be*.

He and Bjorn leaped from the pilings into the boat and he pried with the long sculling oar to shove the *Guld* out of the slip. Once the bow was cleared, he swung the stern around then handed the oar to Bjorn. Now the sails. The mainsail took the breeze and at the tiller he strained to see the rowboat, but the *Flicka* was between the *Guld* and the upside-down craft, only a quarter of a mile away. His father would have to take in sail right now or he would either run by or ram Heinie. He and Stephan were sailors born; they had to know what to do at a time like this. They did. The *Flicka's* mainsail slackened and her keel settled into the water.

"*Hang on Heinie!*" Aaron remembered Heinie had begged him to do just that when he'd been lying helpless with dysentery in a cold, wet wild plum thicket during the War. The crack and boom and smoke of battle had been relentlessly encroaching, but Heinie had taken off his own underwear to make diapers for him and had tended him like a baby. Heinie really had only that one failing—a weakness for women. Who knew, maybe that was something he couldn't help. He would find a girl some day who was of a like temperament and he'd straighten up and be a family man. Still, he'd acted like a gentleman this afternoon, though everyone present had seen that he was strongly attracted to Mandy.

The wind was whipping the bay now, as it almost always did when you were in trouble with a boat or nets. Wind was the thing about commercial fishing that scared Liza so—it scared him. They were close enough to hear their father say something to Stephan.

"Slow us down," Aaron directed Bjorn, gesturing toward the sails. Closing the gap, they could see Stephan and their father steady the *Flicka* with centerboard and anchor. The slim hull bobbed a few feet from the upset skiff. One of the men threw a line to the figure clinging to the capsized boat. Heinie would be safe now.

"Scull us close," he told Bjorn. "Pa and Uncle Stephan are pulling Heinie into the *Flicka*."

When the two gill net boats bumped each other, Aaron lashed their bows together. He could see that the drenched man lying face down in the bottom of the *Flicka* was not moving. Lord, were they too late to help the comrade who'd saved his and Henning's skins more than once by his guts and cunning? *Oh, Henning!*

He vaulted from the *Guld* into the *Flicka*. "Has Heinie had too much water or has he swooned?" he inquired anxiously of his father, but the older man was gazing out to sea in uncomprehending shock. Aaron bent over the long, wide-shouldered form in the blue army tunic, then his knees buckled and his rump slid down the curved hull of the *Flicka* to the floor.

"Pa!" an ascending scream rose and he clamped his jaws on it, filtering the words through his teeth. *"Pa, where is Heinie?"* Then he scrambled wildly to his feet again.

August Greutzmacher's fingernails were torn back and bleeding, but Aaron saw they were grooving the pine boards. At the sound of Aaron's voice, the elderly man began to convulse and he struggled to push himself up with his arms. His head bounced hard on the boards of the floor when he fell and his battered nose hemorrhaged. He tried to rise and failed again, succeeding only in turning his distorted, bloodied face to Aaron.

"Heinie's under the skiff. Oh, Aaron, I tipped it over." His head dropped a final time and a tremor ran through his body before it was still.

God! Why were they all standing there? "Start rubbing August," Aaron told his granduncle, stifling another outcry that surged from below his breastbone.

"Pa, get the grappling hook from Bjorn. I have to find Heinie."

He had to let himself down into the cold, suffocating embrace of the bay before the undertow rolled Heinie away. He stepped to the starboard bow and tied the free end of the mooring rope around his waist. His father handed him a three-pronged, forged iron hook with a coil of rope attached. "Pa, you and Stephan give me a minute under the rowboat then pull me up."

Stephan left the inert body of August and stood at the ready until their father groggily joined him at the rail.

Aaron perched on the gunwale, preparing to let himself into the water, feet first. Like many another who spent his working life on the water, he'd never learned to swim. He gripped his nose and mouth with his left hand and let the weight of his body pull him under.

Propelling himself with his right hand which held the grapple, he came up quickly under the small, flat hull. He flailed his arm, taking care not to foul himself in the skiff's anchor line. There was no one under the boat. He paddled out and the old men hauled him to the surface. Gulping air, he clung to the rail of the *Flicka* and his father and Stephan gripped him with beseeching hands.

Bjorn leaped into the *Flicka* and pleaded, weeping hoarsely, "Aaron, please get back in the boat. You can't help Heinie."

Stephan began to work again on August Greutzmacher, but their father stumbled to a fish box and sat with his head in his hands, moaning.

"I have to try again," Aaron cried, gasping and shaking from chill and emotional reaction. "Bjorn, help me to the stern. Heinie has to be down there somewhere." He overhanded aft with Bjorn moving ahead of him in the boat. Their father had never let go of the mooring line and he staggered to the rail to help.

Eight feet down in the undertow, the limp body of the ex-soldier crabbed over the rocks abaft the *Flicka's* stern. Aaron took a deep breath and went down and hooked an iron prong of net retriever in the trousers' belt of his friend.

16

A Moving Shaft of Sun

After the noon meal of this late summer day, Leander skirted the impending crisis in the coopershop and went to the beach to mend nets. He reeled the last of the whitefish nets onto the blades of a wide-armed spool and stretched a section of torn herring net between two posts. Except for their proximity to the cooling green waves, the task of net patching would have been tedious woman work. Battling the rolling and sometimes pitching bay with rudder, sail and net—that was what a man was born to do.

A yell of pain from the cooperage cut through his day dreaming. Aaron had burned himself again. For two weeks the would-be cooper had striven fruitlessly with the used equipment and carelessly cured stave blanks they'd bought in Green Bay. And for the same fortnight, Bjorn had daily chopped up ruined pine barrels for firewood, These last days, Olaf and August Greutzmacher had been in the shop, but with Aaron firing, the barrels had still spurted water.

With fall coming on, they'd soon gamble herring nets set in the storms of the autumnal equinox where the struggle would be with wind and water, not with the grinding labor of hand-crafting kegs. How had he ever considered letting Aaron be forever stuck ashore? But they had to have barrels; if their source of containers ever dried up, they'd have to go farming.

Leander swung his gaze to encompass a bay full of fish, three houses still unfinished for the winter, boats beached for repairs, tattered sails spread on dune grass and juniper, and cords of firewood standing tall and green behind the clearing. What had he done? Why hadn't his family told him to go to Hades with his plan of building a new settlement in one summer?

Sounds of rage and frustration came again from the shop behind him. He could no longer put off what he must do. Fingering his intricately carved cedar needle, he made his way between creeping hemlocks to the log cooperage. Close to the building, he barely dodged a flaming half-made keg flung out of the door by Aaron.

His son saw him and sent a look of defeat and rage behind the cask. "I can not make the barrels you want!" he cried.

"Then I do not ask you!" Leander flared at his blackened, sweat-soaked offspring. "We'll all quit! We'll work in Spalding's sawmill; we can even take up farmland on the Bay de Noc Road."

"Pa! You know we're fishermen," Aaron shot back angrily.

"Then we'll order more kegs from that robber in Lower Michigan as long as he will sell them to us, no matter how much we have to pay."

Olaf came out with a bucket of water and doused the spoiled barrel and resumed his seat on a stave-shaping buck in the shop.

"I've been trying to tell Aaron he should let August do the firing," he said, indicating the middle-aged German who was loosening a separate year's growth from an ash hoop-plank gripped at one end between logs high on the wall.

Leander let himself down on a stack of stave slabs. "If we cannot make our own salt fish barrels, we cannot," he reiterated.

Aaron bent over the hewn workbench and banged his fists on it. "We must finish what we started!" he cried. "This is crazy—thousands of men are making barrels with less equipment than we have. The world turns on barrels." He turned to August Greutzmacher. "Is that not so?"

"Leander?" There was an excited query in August's pale blue eyes.

"You work in Herr Braun's coopershop sometimes?" Leander asked.

"Ya, I now and then fire and do other jobs when Heinie was in the war."

"You fire now?"

The stonemason's great shoulders and hands pulled him into a perpetual stoop. He looked around the room and chose his words carefully. "You ask me, I tell you. I fire and make headings. Olaf can dress staves and hoops. We make kegs."

Leander grinned in spite of himself and handed the speaker a bundle of thinned staves. August fitted them in a truss-hoop until every stave held to the other like a keystone. Each man in the sweltering building drew a long breath, hoping, doubting, waiting.

August turned to Olaf. "You put fresh shavings in fire can?" he asked, pointing to the two-foot-high sheet iron cylinder standing upright in the fireplace. "I put on love hoop and quarter hoops and we try the fire."

When the cylinder was red-hot, August lifted the barrel over it with the flaring, unconfined ends down. Presently, he slid feeling, calloused hands down the staves then returned the inside-charred, hot barrel to the half circle cut in the front of the cooper's bench and pulled the hot, smoking stave ends in place with a rope and pulley.

Leander saw his sons straighten and assume hoping smiles. August put on the last of eight plaited-end hoops and made chimb grooves inside the keg ends with a sharp tool. "Hand me the heads," he said, and Aaron handed him four precisely doweled and beveled half circles.

"*This one must not leak.*" Leander told himself, unaware that he was speaking aloud, "If it does, we quit this foolishness."

The keg was finished. Aaron poured a bucket of water in it and August fitted the final half heading. They all stood there, wornout and dubious, awaiting seepage or knife-like stream. Aaron shouted, picked up the dry cask and said, "Here Olaf," and tossed it to his brother.

Gleefully, Olaf lobbed it back.

Aaron set the barrel on the workbench and rearranged the taut muscles of his face into a smile. "Well I guess we know now who the coopers are," he said, caressing the smooth, still dry container. "If they've made one salt fish keg, they can make five hundred more. Where is Bjorn?"

"Why? He's clearing land back of the night pasture. If you want him, I'll get him," Olaf offered.

"You do that," Aaron said with the first enthusiasm he'd shown since Heinie's drowning. "We'll have a piece of bread and I'll take him back with me to the white pines and we'll cut stave bolts for a couple of hours. We'll cut the biggest pine of all. You'll hear it crash."

"I'll split stave slabs myself and pile them straight and true for next year," Olaf promised. "I'm sure that's where our trouble's been."

Leander, watching his oldest son walk off with scarcely a limp to fetch Bjorn, mentally saluted Carl Nicholson for the ingenious boot.

August cleared his throat several times then spoke up, "I say before, but maybe no one heard me, Heinie's papa gets his stave slabs from Thorwald Olson in Marinette. What do you think?

"We could put the *Guld* in the water and go down there," Aaron said.

"That we will," Leander agreed gratefully. "I'll tell Mama and start caulking the boat." He strode across the brook bridge to the log cabin hulled with pink and purple morning glories and floating like an ark in waves of summer flowers. If Helga was watching him, she'd know by the exuberance of his stride that the coopers had mastered a barrel at last.

He was glad for the good news, for these days he was scarcely able to talk to his wife in a normal tone of voice unless he was impelled by a lively idea. Deep down he knew he was guilty of interferring with the Creator's design, but in her presence he instinctively attempted a transfusion of life from his body to hers. Yet he constantly reminded himself that he, like even the young and strong, would one day be old and dying. And he'd not have the incalculable benefit of Helga's patient and happy spirit.

He arranged a carefree mien on his face and in his voice and entered the cottage. "A real barrel!" he exulted to the women sitting at the table preparing vegetables for drying. The boys have made a good one!"

Liza's face glowed with relief and she ran out the door with Naomi and the terrier. Through the window, he saw Aaron embrace her triumphantly on the bridge.

"I'm so happy for you all, Leander." Helga held out her hand to him and smiled. "They'll make many more, you'll see."

The light of life still in her thin face smote him and he fought down a recurring and whelming urge to wheel, run to the beach and on to Chambers Island, miles across the water. This moment and many more before the winter was over would decide the temper of his manhood. He stood beside his wife and held her head briefly against his side, feeling in anguish the appalling angles of her skull under the warm mound of hair.

Moving to the front window to compose himself, he watched Stephan and Garnet leave the north beach and the new herring net she'd helped him knit and equip with sinkers and cedar floats. Wearing a pair of Stephan's old pants and a sunbonnet, the stooped old lady walked behind her bed-companion. They were a pair!

Then it came to him again; at this time, anything on Johann-nsens' Landing could be spared except Aaron's wife's ex-slave, though it continued to gall him that the old couple were sleeping legally unmarried right in his own house.

But Helga really believed she *had* married Stephan and Garnet that evening in the cow barn at Ephraim. And truly she had. Then why couldn't he let it be and rid himself of the rancor still gnawing his insides? The terrible thing was, he knew; but the certain cure for cancer of the spirit had eluded him again; nor had he found any balm for it like the soothing hands, voice and potion of the scrawny brown woman who hovered over Helga in the long night hours.

Helga too had seen the rejoicing crew converging on her house. "We were going to have those pies for supper," she said when he opened the food safe, looking for a snack; "but now's a better time. No one can make custard pies like Garnet. Leander, quick! Put a pot of coffee on to boil."

The gay, impromptu gathering was manna for soul and body. Helga and Aaron especially seemed to be renewed. Helga squeezed Aaron's hand and that of Naomi who sat at the corner of the table. Her smile lit the room like a moving shaft of sun. "I want you all to remember this day," she told them.

"We will," Bjorn said, half rising from his chair and pointing through the scrim-screened door. "Those Indians are here again. They're waiting for somebody to come out."

"What do they want now?" Leander asked testily. "They've been here every time we turned around all summer."

"Well Leander," Helga reminded, "where did you think Garnet got the maple sugar for these pies?"

"Pa, have you forgot how much you liked the steak from that hind quarter of venison?" Bjorn interrupted. "Maybe we'd better give back that smoked sturgeon we couldn't stop eating, it was so good."

"We'll build a smokehouse and smoke our own," Leander replied.

"Right now, by the look of their baskets, the No-Sah-We-Quets have brought the late blueberries they promised," Aaron noted, rising from the table. "Come, Liza, we'll go and talk to them."

He started to the door then turned back. "Ma, I guess we finished up the pie, but do you have any of those raisin cookies the Indian children like so much?"

."You get the berries," Leander told him then; "I'll bring the cookies. Do you see my friend Wan-Dah-Sega there?" He'd begun to feel a kinship with the elderly Potawatomi he'd met in the April storm.

"If it's all right with Ma, I'm going to try to get them to come in the house this time," Aaron proposed. "They asked us into their hut when Bjorn and I went there to see if they could find us some berries for canning."

"Are the little girls and the baby with them?" Helga wanted to know. "I've made something for them. Aaron, I think it's a good idea; why don't you and Liza go and bring them all in the house?"

"Leander," she went on, "maybe you and Stephan could help Garnet clear the table and set it again. Get out the good dishes. It's been a long time since we had two parties hand-running."

17

When Words Are Worthless

Joy and loving-kindness welled in Liza at the sight of Wood Fern No-Sah-We-Quet. Of the two young Potawatomi women, Fern was most likely to talk and she knew a little English from working one summer for a commercial fisherman's wife at Manitowoc. The girl's comeliness—straight nose, smooth nutmeg skin and eyes like spring water over brown rocks—was illuminated for Liza because of her own Indian ancestry. Today Liza felt a special kinship with the slim young mother, for pregnancy was delicately lifting Fern's buckskin shift.

Only the two brothers, their wives and children had occupied the big dugout canoe on this trip down shore. They stood now on the beach by the *Guld*'s slip with three pecks of blueberries in bark baskets. In the excitement of meeting and greeting, two mongrel feists sprang from the beached craft and set upon the terrier, Tippy, who'd followed his family. When Naomi began to scream for the safety of her best loved companion, Fern's husband Jacob, snatched up his agressive male, knelt at the pilings and held him under the deep water.

Naomi clutched Liza frantically about the thighs and shrieked for an end to the strange dog's mistreatment. Aaron was looking out to the island, purposely unseeing, talking as best he could with Jacob's brother Alec.

Liza took his arm. "You can't let that man kill the dog!"

Aaron drew away and spoke in the first angry tone he'd used in speaking to her. "We mind our own business. Tell Naomi to shut up."

Jacob No-Sah-We-Quet threw the nearly drowned dog into the canoe and the female jumped in after her mate. Liza kept a hand over Naomi's mouth for fear the child would blurt out, "Ye be a bad man," as she had to Leander.

Were Indians always cruel to their animals? Liza wondered as she moved half-hesitantly now to speak with Wood Fern and her sister, Rose-That-Heals. Rose's baby Timmy was full of brown energy after surviving Papa Johannsen's treatment at the camp here in the April storm. Timmy's sister Martha and Fern's three-year-old Marie instinctively herded him from the edge of the slip.

"We're that glad to see you," Liza told the women warmly. We want you to come up to the house this time." Then pointing to Aaron, "His mama wants to see your younguns. She made something for them."

Even with a further direct invitation from Aaron, the Potawatomi held back from going up to the house. "Sell berries, go home," Jacob maintained.

Liza saw that her husband was unusually distressed by the Indians' unwillingness. "Our mother is sick, very bad," he explained slowly and earnestly. "She'd been sewing for your children. I was going to bring the presents up to your place if you didn't come with the berries."

"We go home."

"This means a lot to her. You don't have to stay long. Come, come on to the house."

"Fern and Rose have gift too," Jacob announced then. "We know mama sick."

Fern took a pair of fawnskin moccasins trimmed with trade beads worked in her own fern design from her shoulder bag and handed them to Liza.

"Miz No-Wah-We-Quet, they be sartin purty," Liza praised sincerely, passing them back, "but ye must fotch 'em to Mama Johannsen yoreself. Hit'll pleasure her no end."

The blank look on the Potawatomi's faces told Liza that in her eagerness to be hospitable she'd lapsed into mountain talk again. Had the No-Sah-We-Quets understood her at all? They had, but only because Aaron had been translating into plain English behind her back. With relief, she saw that the visitors were picking up the blueberries and admonishing the dogs.

Liza held Naomi by the hand and fell behind the group as they walked past the brook pilings to Helga's flower garden. There the Indian men and Aaron gazed impatiently out to sea while the wren-bird women bent to the sweet scented white Angel's

Trumpets and pointed with delight at the flaming nasturtiums climbing the gill net fence.

Jacob's body spelled wariness as he followed Aaron through the door of the cabin. The Potawatomi were as spooky as young foxes. Bringing up the rear, Liza's glance took in the table Stephan and Garnet had quickly cleared and relaid with Helga's best china sauce dishes and cups together with stewed dried peaches and the raisin cookies Aaron had specified.

In the big kitchen-living room, Aaron told their guests, "This is our mother and our Aunt Garnet; Uncle Stephan, Pa, August and the rest you know already."

"The two Indian men shook hands gravely with their male acquaintances but they ignored the Johannsen womenfolk. When Helga started to rise in a gesture of welcome, Jacob peremptorily waved her down. She smiled at him and turned to Wood Fern, Rose and their children. "I'm so glad to have company," she assured them, holding out both of her thin hands.

Jacob nudged Fern who made a sort of curtsy to her hostess and presented the moccasins. Again Helga's smile was like a light in the room. "Thank you so much; I'll wear them always."

She beckoned Leander to her chair. "Do you see these? Could you please take off those old clodhoppers and put them on my feet? They're the most beautiful slippers I ever saw."

For a moment, Helga wiggled her toes in the exquisitely soft footwear, then her eyes swept the room, looking for someone. "Garnet," she called through the crowd, "would you please go in my bedroom and get the things we made for the little ones?"

Shortly, Garnet laid folded periwinkle velvet garments in her lap.

Oh, my! it struck Liza, Papa Johannsen's going to notice right off that Mama Johannsen has cut up her wedding dress.

He did, he jumped up and cried, "Helga, what did you do?"

Jacob's sharp eyes flashed and the sinews of his body readied themselves. Would Papa Johannsen scare the No-Sah-We-Quets off even before they sat at his table?

Helga hushed her husband with a look and made a come-hither motion to Wood Fern, explaining, "These are for the children." She held up one of three small jackets. "I made them on the machine that sews."

Moved by curiosity and anticipation, the women edged the children up to Helga when they saw that she was presenting the wonderful garments to them.

After the little coats had been tried on with soft murmurs of pleasure, Helga told Leander gaily, "Help me up, I want to sit at the table with our guests."

"Yes, yes," Leander said to the No-Sah-We-Quets, "We'd be proud to have you eat with us."

Jacob's ordering glance swept his group; but Liza read a message on Garnet's face, "Them wild things hain't goin' to set at no table."

For a moment it did look like the Potawatomi were going to grab some food and plop down on the floor. Then Wood Fern, showing her knowledge of white man's ways, slid along the bench behind the table and pulled Rose and the children, still dressed in their jackets, behind her.

Watching the pixie, pecan-skinned children with their straight black hair and snapping jet-brown eyes, Liza was amazed to see that Naomi was indeed a throwback as Garnet had often said. She could have been a cousin to the little Potawatomi girls. That prospect caused her to consider: But how long will it take before they can be sisters? Why is it socially acceptable to be one-fourth Indian (or one-fourth Negro, if you could get away with it), but fullbloods are forever beyond the pale?

The Indian women tentatively bird-fed the peaches and cow's milk to their offspring who spit out the milk and solemnly and steadily consumed cookies.

Aaron was clearly wracking his brain for something to say that Jacob and Alec could relate to with interest when Jacob remarked at last, "Much fish?"

"No," Aaron replied with relief crossing his face. "We fix nets, make barrels and cut wood for the winter."

"Too much work." Jacob shook his head. "So much work is crazy."

With her eyes on her saucer of peaches, Liza knew it was true; the No-Sah-We-Quets would never shackle themselves to a dream as the Johannsens had. Shifting her glance slightly, she observed that Fern and Rose were handling and commenting quietly over one of Helga's flowered bone china sauce dishes. Suddenly it had disappeared and Liza knew it was inside Rose's blouse. At first she was shocked at the theft, then it came to her, what can it matter now to Mama Johannsen?

But it mattered to Jacob; Liza noticed that his sharp eyes had caught the larceny. Abruptly, he stood up, bowed slightly to Leander directly across the table and said, "Many thanks. We go.'' He led his tribe out the door, followed by Aaron, Bjorn, Naomi and herself. Helga leaned on the jamb of the open door and waved as the No-Sah-We-Quets shoved off the beach.

"Well, Bjorn," Aaron said as the Potawatomi's paddles struck deep water, "I guess we still have time to fell that big white pine."

Liza waited a moment, watching Naomi dig in the dune with a driftwood sand shovel the Indian children had left behind. A southwest wind flattened the great waters at her feet so they seemed safe and tranquil. How would it feel to be penned in by hills again? From a child, she'd had a fear of being shut in a closed room and boxed hollows between ridges had vaguely distressed her. Looking out where water and sky met beyond a place Aaron said was Washington Island, the knowledge came; as long as waves lapped or crashed, the best and freest place on earth to be was at the edge of this bounding deep.

But like Helga, her druthers would have kept her on the far side of the bay on the lovely shore of the Wisconsin peninsula they'd left in the spring. Daily that favored land, where fine farms were being cleared, could be seen on the horizon. It would be so good to be farming again, but she knew the Johannsen men would shrivel and die away from the inscrutable fields of wave and reef.

"Come with me to Grandma's glory house," Naomi coaxed at bedtime following the visit of the Potawatomi. The child's tone forced Liza to reproach herself; these darkling trips to the closet Helga had swathed in morning-glory vines had been the only way the child could snatch a few minutes each day from her mother.

For she, who'd been given the personal slave, Garnet, for a wedding present, had subjected herself to prove to Aaron's family that she and her dependents would be no burden in the Johannsens' year of trial. She'd adamantly set herself to keep the Scandinavians' houses, food and clothing as Helga would have, had she been three women and well and strong again. In addition, she was planing the floors of her own house with shards of broken glass, troweling the cracks of Helga's log cabin inside and out with hair lime, sand and bay water and doing the washings.

Through it all, Naomi had seemed unaffected by the neglect. She'd learned to tell from Garnet's comings and goings when Aaron's mother was up and feeling well enough to tell whimsical teaching stories about wildlife, people and places as she sewed or prepared vegetables. Or the youngster would get permission to seek out Olaf at the cooperage where she'd sit on the floor by his stave buck, awaiting a suggestive curl of pine.

"Uncle Olaf," she'd ask, "what do ye think this one is?"

Almost daily, Olaf wove tales that were as puckish as his mother's and he was teaching the child her alphabet and numbers, marking with characoal on stave blanks. "I think you'll be able to read by spring," he'd told her a few days before. "I've already asked Mandy to bring you a reader from town."

This balmiest of summer evenings, Liza and Naomi encountered Garnet and Mama Johannsen making their slow way back from the comfort cubicle situated upbrook a few rods and they were all standing in the starlit yard, gazing up at the shimmering sky. Away from the house, Garnet, like a calico-draped hickory crutch, supported Helga. Now the ill woman attempted to withdraw from her companion and stand on her own. "Garnet, I'll wear you out," she demurred. "I should stay in the house where I belong." Then she impulsively clasped the hand of the brown woman. "But I'd have missed this beautiful night. Isn't it just perfect? We have only a few of these each year up here."

Garnet pivoted herself under Helga's arm so the swaying woman hung again from her reedy frame. "De Lord gib me a strong backbone fer leanin'," she insisted. "Don't ye worry none, Hit'll last ye."

Swiveling her thrown-back head to encompass the full, glittering canopy of night, Naomi pointed to the brilliant polestar and declared, "I'm going to have that one for my own star."

"Ye cain't," Garnet objected promptly. "Hit's tuk, dey all tuk. Dey de shinin' faces of all de folks God tuk to Heaven since He made dat garden with no ice nor snow. 'Sides, dat special one be Enos."

"Who be Enos?"

"He be a good man I had me a long time ago. And ye watch, when Stephan and me're gone. Ye goin' to see two new stars a'glistnin' right up thar a'side a him."

"Will I get a brand new star when I die, even if I be little and don't grow up big?"

"Ye will, my baby, ye will," Garnet promised.

Tonight they'd had another party, a sixteenth year celebration for Bjorn at Mama Johannsen's. Liza had opened the door and stepped out to fling a pan of dishwater on the dusking dune at the edge of the yard. Though it was August, the weather was like

February in the hills of home. Melting sleet pricked her face and she thought: winter has come and it'll last forever; it'll take Mama Johannsen and keep me from having a live baby. Where in all that darkness were the warm hills of Tennessee? It couldn't matter when she'd never see them again.

A whicker recalled her to Johannsens' Landing and by the dim light from the open door on Helga's cabin, she saw the star on the face of the Nicholsons' Sam. The horse and his rider were shrouded in steam. She flung the water and dropped the pan on the stoop. Sam's head was hanging and he braced himself on legs that had dragged a heavy wagon all day. It was strange that the countenance of a much loved horse or dog could be as dear to you as your best friend. Gunnar Nicholson slid off the animal and she caught him with one arm about his shoulder.

"What brings you out in this weather?" she urged him to explain.

"I have to talk to Olaf." The boy loosed himself from her and leaned against Sam's heaving barrel, his face averted from the icy precipitation.

She took his arm again. "Mandy?"

Gunnar nodded mutely.

"I reckon she got hurt someway."

"No, she's got typhoid."

"Bad?"

"She's bad. I brung her all the way from Menominee in the back of the wagon. It took me two days."

"I reckon I'd better get Aaron to come and see the best way to tell Olaf."

Olaf loved sweet Mandy in more ways than most men could know if they outlived a dozen wives. Dear Lord, how could they tell Olaf?

She went to the door and called through the netting, "Aaron, could you step out here a minute?"

He came and he too cried, "Mandy!" at the sight of Gunnar and Sam standing in the pelting rain. "Is she hurt?" he continued, his voice rising in alarm.

"She's got typhoid bad," Liza told him, sparing Gunnar from repeating his explanation.

"God, how can we tell a thing like that to Olaf?" Aaron asked through gritted teeth. "I'd rather shoot him!"

"I'll take Sam to the barn," Liza told the men. "Aaron, you must break the news to Olaf."

"You can't take Sam!" Gunnar opposed fiercely. "Ma's gone to Green Bay to tend Grandma Jasperson. I got to get back to Mandy. Pa don't know how to tend her right."

"You can use Buck," Aaron broke in and took Sam's letdown checkrein from Gunnar.

"Liza, you tie Sam to the bar in the old shed," Aaron directed when the boy nodded. "Can you bridle Buck over his halter and bring him from the barn? I'll get Gunnar some dry clothes from our cabin. But first I'll do what I have to do."

Buck's stall in the log barn was clean and dry, a peaceful place to hide from pain and heartbreak. Guided by only the barest diffused light from a small window, Liza spoke to the gelding and slid in beside him. At the manger, she set the small of her back against the horse's warm shoulder to ease the ache for Olaf that ran down her spine and the backs of her legs.

She'd untied the claybank's rope and was backing him with her hand pressing against his soft breast when she saw Olaf's face in the glimmer of the four-sided candle lantern he held in the faint rectangle of the open door.

"I need Kate," he said. "I'm going with Gunnar."

She fumbled for Buck's bridle hanging in the corner. It was there, but where were the words she must say to Olaf? "Olaf," she began finally, "thar be a time when words be of no use atall."

He'd hung the lantern and was in the stall with the black mare. "Liza," he said over the plank divider, "I know you got a better way of praying than most of us except Ma. I'd be beholden to you if you prayed for Mandy."

"Olaf, your mama once told me a fisherman's wife was a walking prayer. You can depend on it. I'll hold you both before the Lord, night and day."

Olaf had backed Kate out and was bridling her in the alley a horse length away. "Liza, I have to tell you, Mandy and I were going to let you and Aaron know on Sunday that we'd have to move our wedding date up from October."

"She's not...?"

"No. We just need to be married. It's got so I can't trust myself, and she's too young for that."

Liza pressed her open mouth into the side of Buck's warm muzzle, smothering spasms of sobs. Good, sweet, beautiful Mandy!

18

My Children Are All Dead

Facing away from oblique missiles of rain, Aaron held the lantern for Olaf and Gunnar Nicholson as they mounted the barebacked horses at the door of their parents' cabin. He knew their mother stood, drooping with dismay, in the open door behind them.

What was Bjorn saying to Gunnar with a detaining hand on Buck's bridle? "It's settled then? I'm to come in the morning when Sam's rested and help you with the dray line?"

In the doorway their father stiffened with a disappointment verging on rage. "Bjorn," he demanded, "what are you saying?"

"I'm going into business with Gunnar," Bjorn stated flatly.

"We cannot spare you with Olaf gone."

Gunnar broke into the argument, "I got to fetch a load of flour from Marinette by the end of the week. If Olaf can make out with nursing Mandy, I'll pull out of the Forks by noon tomorrow." The events of the past two days had made a man of Gunnar, even his voice had deepened.

"I'll be there in plenty of time," Bjorn assured him, holding onto Buck as though this chance to escape the fishery would fly off into thin air.

"Seven o'clock," Gunnar stressed. "Before we make the long run, we got a typhoid coffin to take up the river to the cemetery in the new hearse body Pa made for the old wagon."

"We could use our team on this trip and let Sam and Gert have a rest."

Gunnar gave Bjorn a glancing, superior look. "I guess fishermen have a lot to learn about freighting."

"Buck and Kate'll do anything we say."

"They'd be pooped out before we were loaded to come home."

Aaron's mind was rocking and his legs were weak. So, after all his threats, Bjorn was leaving; and who knew when Olaf would be home? It was all over—the fine plans the Johannsens had made following the War had been shot in the head. All there'd be left for a crew, beside himself, would be three old men.

"Well, Ma, I guess we'll be going," Olaf said to his mother. Don't worry about me, I'll stay with Mandy as long as she needs me, then I'll be back."

At Olaf's words, Aaron scolded himself: I'm a fool to concern myself about success when Olaf probably faces the end of the world: I should be glad we have four men left, two for coopering and two for cutting a wagon trail through to the Bay de Noc Road.

He was about to say to the riders, "Godspeed. Take care," when a commotion erupted behind his parents in the lamplight. Where were Liza, Stephan, Garnet? What was going on?

Stephan stepped between the elder Johannsens, and Garnet, turbanned and shawled, followed him with a bundle. Garnet couldn't leave their mother!

"I reckon ye best fix for me to set in front," the leprechaun-faced lady said to Olaf. "I be goin' with ye fer a couple of days and show ye jist what to do. I tuk keer a many a fever."

Aaron saw that his brother had been hoping for the old lady's appearance. Olaf slid back to Kate's loins and Stephan boosted up his gnome-like partner.

Liza came out and they all stood in the dooryard in the wintry rain. Garnet reached down to Stephan. "Ye got hit hall locked in yore haid?"

"Aye," he brought her gnarled fingers to his lips. "I'll see to Helga with Liza's help; but you come back, Mama, come back."

More than a week before, the lonesome bawl of a freighting ox had fired Aaron with the notion of making a wagonway from the fishery docks out to the new Bay de Noc Road less than a mile away. The ox had surely been draying on the sixteen-foot-wide slash that had just been cut through timber across country from Menominee to Cedar Forks. It was worth your life to ride on the stage and freighting trace, but it was a road through the trackless wilderness and wheels had rolled, lurched and bogged on it all summer.

This morning in the wet daybreak, he stood by the *Silver*

Guld's mooring post and noted that the lake, flattened by a southwest wind, was a ready-made highway with no swamps or stumps. Why then was he going off past the end of his garden with an ax over his shoulder to blaze a wagon road on land? Because, though she lay like a sheet of glass this morning, the lake could not be trusted.

He turned from the beach trail where Bjorn had ridden off on tough and lanky Sam before anyone was up that morning. At the edge of the potato patch, clipping off two-inch aspens at the ground and tossing them aside, Aaron began to mark a broad pike, for that was what it would be in time. Swiftly he cleared a path through the gray-green aspen thicket growing on an arm of the old Indian clearing.

His heart wasn't in it; as much as he hated coopering, he'd rather have been in the shop with August, or better still with his father and Stephan bobbing in the *Guld*, setting whitefish nets. With Henning, Heinie, Bjorn and Olaf gone, he felt more strongly then ever the need to be with other men.

But they must have a road, a passable wagon track to haul a pine box to the burgeoning burial ground up the river from Cedar Forks when the time came, and a smooth access by sleigh to bring in a midwife for Liza. Twice a year on this northern shore, water-side residents were tightly apprehensive—at freeze-up in early winter and at break-up in early spring; and there was no guarantee of winter ice thick enough to bear traffic. Their mother's spark of life was sure to go out at one of those difficult times. Without a wagon or sleigh road, she'd have to be buried on the beach like a sailor lost from a storm-sunk schooner.

When it had been cut, corduroyed and leveled, others would use his tote road too—Indians, loggers, fishermen and would-be farmers. Numerous fisheries and fishing camps were mushrooming now on the long west shore of Green Bay. From a boat anchored out by the nets in the lake, you could see hopeful neighbors carving homestead clearings as the Johannsens were doing. Next winter on the ice, the Johannsen men—God knew how many would be left by then—would meet and talk with their fellow gill netters. But the womenfolk on shore would be isolated from each other by an ocean of trees, extending to the west, north and south, and a fickle deep heaving to the horizon on the east.

Leaving the patch of young aspen, he gashed the heavy bark of a hemlock, and moving with the warm rays of the sun in his wake, blazed a curve that would miss the larger trees in the grove.

A few more rods of the hemlock stand and he encountered a black ash swale narrow enough to be spanned by felling nearby trees across it. He took off his good leather land boots—which must be saved at all costs, waded through the slimy, stagnant water and came up onto a ridge of twenty or thirty giant white pines like those behind the fishery clearing.

Leaving his own land now, he set himself to steer a course between or around merchantable timber. Cruising the cambered oval knob of pine both ways, his tender bare toes scrunching three centuries of damp, resin-scented pine needles, he saw that a long barrier of cedar swamp blocked his way. He leaned against a six-foot pine bole, rising with storied green limbs to the sky and rooted so nothing but the steel blades of greedy white men could dislodge it. He was tempted to turn back. Spalding or some other timberman would use his road to exploit these grand trees.

Had he come a quarter of a mile? He contemplated the dense cedar swamp, then he wasted half an hour, hiking to the right and left, hoping to find a way to circumnavigate it. He sat on a fallen snag to ease the charley-horse in his leg. Why hadn't he brought a piece of bread and one of his mother's canning jars full of fresh water? Well, if the fishery was to be land-liberated by wagon road, he must get up and explore a course north by west through the jungle. He must push through hummock, water and deadfall, cutting a swath through the massed infantry of late summer mosquitoes and ranks of low-limbed cedar. The only real clue to the whereabouts of the dray road he sought was the remembered bawl of the ox.

He put his boots on again, though it would take an hour of work at night, greasing them to keep them from being ruined, and blazed straight ahead. Before long, he came upon a mass of downed trees laced with rank blackberry briers, but it was low enough to give him the sun again and he corrected his course by a few degrees. Once into it, the windfall became a natural trap for a sailor and he fought to excape the snaring tentacles of roots and limbs. He fell on his back in the muck, and the winged enemy held him there, buzzing and stabbing.

He crawled out on his hands and knees through hoops of branches driven into the mud and feared in panic, when the sun was momentarily obscured, that he had lost his direction. A greenbrier lashed him across the shoulders and neck and bound him with barbed vine. He bloodily extricated himself and proceeded, skirmishing with the mosquitoes with one hand and marking trail with the other.

It was hopeless, there'd never be a road out of Johannsens' Landing except on the beach where there were swamps also, and great shoves of ice to impede travel in late winter and spring. Even if he did find the Bay de Noc Road, a thousand trees, laid bole to bole, whould not pave this swamp.

Out of the island of cedar at last, bushed and deadlocked with himself, he sat with his back against the trunk of a towering sugar maple in one of those small, inexplicably grassy forest clearings. He could do either of two things now; he could keep going onward for what he judged to be a quarter of a mile or he could turn around in his tracks, fight his way back through that hellish mass of blowdowns and go home—if the sun stayed out and he'd left a discernable backtrack.

A fox was yipping on his trail now, the first sound of an animal he'd heard except for the scolding jays and blackbirds. Why was the fox following him? Was it rabid, smelling his warm blood? It was the time of year for mad dogs and such. He rose with ax in hand but the onrushing canine was Tippy, wet, scratched and happy. The small dog leaped almost to his shoulder, and he caught him in his arms and hugged him.

With company brightening his day, he slogged and chopped on through mixed lowland timber, mainly straight white ash the right size for corduroy. Tippy ran ahead, gleefully flushing the undergrowth for menacing animals or snakes. Suddenly the terrier treed a gray squirrel and Aaron ran forward, for the bushy-tailed fellow would streak off for high ground.

The squirrel deftly eluded Tippy, but Aaron caught sight of his banner tail slithering between the trees and followed, crashing through brush maple and jumping rotten tree trunks. There it was! A ridge of hard maple interspersed with beech trees lay ahead. Gunnar said the new road had been charted to take advantage of such high land, even if it was the long way around. His legs were slack with anticipation; this had to be it, the location of the bawling ox.

Between the frantic trailing yips of the dog, he heard a new sound, the clunk of wood-spoked wheels and the jingle of harness. He scrambled on, forgetting to mark his track, and all at once, he was standing, panting and soaked with swamp water and sweat, in the middle of a rude trace. Sam and Gert were plodding toward him a few rods up the road. Sam recognized him at once and whickered, alerting Bjorn where he sat nodding on the board seat of the wagon with Gunnar. "Brother!" Bjorn yelled. "Where did you come from?"

Aaron pulled out his shirttail and wiped perspiration mixed with the blood drawn by slain mosquitoes from his face. The tender skin around his ears burned like salted wounds. He was using a branch of maple to fan an opening in the swarm of insects that had followed him to high ground, when the wagon jolted abreast.

The angry stingers hadn't found Bjorn on his perch yet. He said jauntily, "Well, Aaron, I guess you found something besides a trail between here and the bay."

"I brought these critters out here to keep you and Gunnar company on your tiresome trip," Aaron joked in reply.

Too late, he remembered the question that had been on the tip of his tongue when Bjorn interrupted; but the answer was already on Gunnar's face. "Mandy's no better?" he asked the boy belatedly.

Gunnar's always taut countenance was drawn tighter and his steely blue eyes had faded somehow. "Pa cried in our bed in the barn last night," he said. "I can tell by that how things are."

"Olaf?" Aaron had to know.

"Olaf will die too," Gunnar told him bluntly.

Wearing a disbelieving, I-don't-know-what-you're-talking-about expression, Bjorn jumped down from the wagon and blurted irrelevantly, "Here, I'll rub you with some of this insect dope Gunnar's Pa made. It'll get you back to the bay with a skinfull of blood."

Aaron signaled Bjorn with his eyebrows, and in the silence resulting, Gunnar mentioned, "I'm going to send Ma a telegram from Menominee. I should've done it the day Mandy got sick, but she wouldn't let me. It'll take four days for Ma to get here from Green Bay by stage."

Aaron stepped up to the wagon and shook Gunnar's hand with a grip that articulated his well wishes. Bjorn climbed up over the wheel to the seat of the cumbersome handmade vehicle and drove off with a boy who had grown up in two days. Bjorn had better do some maturing in a hurry or Gunnar, smaller but fired with purpose, would do it for him. Then it came to him that Bjorn had only begun to talk of going to sea when their mother became ill.

When Aaron returned to the snarl of uprooted trees, he chopped an aisle across it, meanwhile calculating a schedule that would enable him to do the work of two men. There was one exception to his Spartan plan—when the trail was cut horse-wide all the way through, he'd take time and walk on to Cedar Forks and see what was going on.

When he'd hacked a trail through bog, brush and blowdown to the hardwood ridge, it was noon of the second day following his meeting with the boys. He sat under a spreading, limber-limbed beech, drank cold coffee, ate the corn pone Liza said would stick to his ribs better than white bread and looked back at the beginnings of a road his father had said was impossible. Path, trail, road, highway—the same sequence held all over the world. The man who made a trail left a monument sometimes enduring for centuries.

It had rained all night and the weather was balmy-cool with a breeze lifting the maple leaves. He got up, hid his ax and started off to the sawmill village, stepping briskly in the wheel tracks. Coming back, he'd be riding Buck and leading Kate. With feed scarce and costly, Carl Nicholson could not feed an idle team a day more than necessary.

The Nicholsons' four room house, warped from having been built of green lumber, rested on pilings in the hastily cleared swamp south of the juncture of the Little Cedar River with the Big Cedar River. Carl Nicholson sat on the uncovered, elevated stoop, carving a chair post. Before Aaron could ask about Mandy, the girl's father shook his head and said, "Well, Aaron, you're here. Olaf is inside with Mrs. Eckberg. Ay call 'em. Ay don't dast go inside, nor do you."

Mrs. Eckberg, who was that? Then Aaron realized he'd heard Garnet called by Stephan's surname.

Olaf spoke through the milky marquisette on the door, but Aaron could see that his tanned and fit brother had become gaunt and pale. He looked startlingly like their mother in her extremity. Had Gunnar spoken in foreboding omniscience? Was Olaf sick already? No, it took ten days or two weeks to come down with typhoid, though he might have come in contact with someone when he called on Mandy two weeks before.

Cedar Forks, or Cedar River as some folks called the village, was riddled with the infection. It was said three Swedes lay in fever and filth on pallets on the floor of a small closed back room of a boardinghouse. They suffered, untended, with their slopjars running over, crawling to the door when they could to drag in food and water thrust at them.

There'd been four hopeful young immigrant Swedes, but one had died and nobody really knew who he was or where he'd come from. The mill had supplied a rough coffin and Mandy and Gunnar had washed his face, combed his hair, folded his hands and hauled him up to the forest cemetery.

Suddenly Aaron knew where Mandy had picked up whatever it was that had caused her to get typhoid. He drove the thought from his mind and cast about for something comforting or helpful to say to his brother through the scrim door. Should he ask, "Olaf, what do you need? How is Mandy? Can I do something?" Yes, but his voice must carry, in addition, the message, "Olaf, I love you and Mandy."

After that Olaf spoke and his voice was dead-toned with weeping, dammed back. "Aaron, my children are all dead. I'll never walk and talk with Isaac and Reuben and Abigail Amanda." He separated the names lovingly, and Aaron's heart broke for the strong sons and pretty daughter Olaf would never see.

"Mandy's very sick?"

"I never saw a fever as high as hers, nor did Aunt Garnet. We keep her body packed in cold wet cloths, but her skin is parching. Her head aches so hard, she can't talk."

"We need a doctor!" Aaron exclaimed in angry frustration, barely concealed. "Curse this wild land!"

"He couldn't do much more than we're doing. Gunnar got a doctor when Mandy came down sick in Marinette. He came to her where she laid in the back of the wagon."

"Didn't he do anything for her?"

"He gave Gunnar some medicines and told him how to take care of her. He didn't know of anyone in town who would take in a typhoid case, so they had to come on home."

Two days in a springless lumber wagon! One day, God willing, there'd be a better way to travel, smooth pikes with steam carriages rolling on them and a railroad into the wilderness. There was talk now of stringing a telegraph line between Menominee and the mouth of the Big Cedar, following the new tote road. With a message by wire, he and Olaf could have brought Mandy home in the rocking chair *Flicka* in one day of fair wind.

"Just a minute," Olaf broke in. He'd stepped back and was talking with Garnet, arguing.

Then turning to Aaron again, he said, "There is one thing you can do, take Aunt Garnet home to Ma."

Now Aaron remembered that Olaf had said, *Aunt* Garnet, from the time their Uncle Stephan had taken her into his bed. "How will you manage till Mandy's mother comes?" he asked his brother.

"She'll be here tomorrow or the next day. I just want to be alone with Mandy till then. I've got a cot in her room."

Ah, now that Mandy's body was being scorched by the very breath of death, no one thought it verboten for Olaf to look after her like a baby. The ways of the world were passing strange.

Soon Aaron could hear Garnet advising Olaf, "Do lak de doctor say. Keep on goin' with de cold packs. Gib her medicine in de fresh milk her daddy brings. Don't, nohow, put your hands up to yore mouth lessen ye woish in carbolic first."

"Do you think it's all right to take Aunt Garnet home?" Aaron asked the tall, sad-faced Swede on the door stoop.

"If Olaf says," Carl Nicholson replied, his voice toneless with fatality. "Dorcas'll be here soon."

The side door of the house opened, and turning his head, Aaron saw Garnet emerge with a wooden bucket. The breeze carried the smell of carbolic acid to him. She crawled under the tilting stoop and dragged out a bundle, the same package she'd carried when she left the Landing in the rain with Olaf. Her hair had been trimmed short, almost to the skull.

He moved past the corner of the house, toward her, "Aunt Garnet?"

"Stay 'way from me. I git in de woodshed and shuck my clothes and woish out de Devil's work. Git de horses, Olaf say I go home to yore mama."

He fetched Buck and Kate from the pole pen by the slab shack of a barn and waited, talking uncomfortably and pointlessly with Carl Nicholson. When Garnet came out of the woodshed, she was dressed in Stephan's pants and shirt. Carrying her discarded clothing at arm's length, she went through the stumpy back yard to the hearth where Dorcas Nicholson kept her soap kettle and started a fire. There, poking and muttering, she burned the garments she'd worn in the sickroom. Finally, she dipped her hands and shoes in the solution in the bucket.

Aaron handed the bridle reins to the grieving cobbler on the porch, stepped up to the door and called, "Olaf?"

Olaf came from the bedroom and said, "Goodbye, Aaron. Tell Ma I'm a good nurse and not to worry."

The only thing Aaron could think of to say was, "Do the best you can; I'll be back day after tomorrow."

Riding with Garnet along the treeless sawdust street toward the looming forest, he had the eerie feeling that he was riding away from Henning again at the Upper Morningstar Baptist church-yard. But this time he was forsaking a living brother at the grave of his lost hope.

19

One Day the Wind Will Blow My Name

Bundled to the ears like a farmer, Leander stood on shore by the *Guld*'s slip and watched the gale-driven bay. You could count on at least one good blow each December and this was the first. He peered through the spyglass but heaving breakers prevented him from seeing the area of their gill net set. There was really no use to look; with that wind, the herring nets were headed for the Door of Death, Porte des Morts, into Lake Michigan. Weeks of work, knitting and stringing, could be lost.

The rampaging wind struck through his mackinaw and he was more irritated at his frailty than at the knifing chill. How could a man, who'd worked bareheaded and barehanded on the North Sea, be so cold? Could worry and heartbreak thin your blood?

Soon Olaf came from Garnet's breakfast table and stood, far-away-silent, beside him where the *Guld* pitched and bumped against coils of old rope hung on the pilings. Olaf raised the collar of his navy blue wool sailor's jacket and pointed mutely to the turbulent clouds charging over the forest to the cold green sea.

"*Say something, Olaf*," Leander cried in his mind. "Say, 'it's a bad blow, say that's the end of those nets.'"

But Olaf stared at the surf, determinedly voiceless, as he had been since the death of Mandy three months before.

"Speak to me, Olaf," Leander's heart pleaded. "Your mother says you talk with her behind the closed door of the room where she lies dying. August told me you teach Naomi, as always, in the coopershop. Communicate with me, Olaf, give me something besides a flick of your hand or a nod of your head."

Standing close, fogged in by disappointment and storm, he shared the pent grief and frustration of his son. But this brooding

108

silence had to stop or Olaf would walk right off the end of the bowsprit one day. Could he say, "Olaf, I know exactly how you feel?" No, he could not, for Olaf was standing there in the flesh, the dear progeny of his loins; and there were still Aaron, Anna and Bjorn and, one day, their childrens' children. There'd be no grandsons now from Olaf—his offspring had not even died aborning. He'd not held one small scrap of himself in his arms.

Then in a sudden mindless attempt at shocking some audible response from Olaf, he said, "I think I'll take the *Guld* and go out there and see what's going on. I'll put another anchor on the nets."

When Olaf failed to answer, he cried out, and at first he thought it had been aloud, "We'll both go, we'll fight the sea together." But Olaf's face showed his preoccupation and his, Leander's, thoughts ran on. Olaf, you and I, we're the only ones suffering so. We're kin beyond father and son.

But conscience accosted him and he remembered guiltily that in their own group, August Greutzmacher, Liza and Garnet had suffered much bereavement. But their love had not been as deep as his and Olaf's; that was the answer. Some people loved with only part of their being. As he did? He groaned inwardly and self-censure broke over him like the combers clawing at the cedar point up shore. Lord, there'd never been a time when he loved anyone better than Leander Johannsen.

No, that was not true; he loved Olaf this minute as only a father can love a good and pleasing son. *Olaf, oh Olaf, how can I help you?* Then it came to him what he must do at the moment. He loosed the pound boat's mooring rope, jumped over the bow, seized the long sculling oar and pried powerfully against the pilings of the slip. "I go," he said. "I go to the nets."

As Leander hoped it would, that maneuver caused Olaf's spirit to leave the grave on the bank of the Big Cedar. "No, Pa!" he objected, and vaulting high and wide, landed in the craft and forcibly took the oar. "Pa," Olaf was talking again; he was talking! "Pa, I'll behave. Come we'll go in the net shed and mend nets. We'll need 'em."

Leander's mind flipped like a stunned sturgeon; the sails of his reason iced in the chilling wind and his mind refused to reverse itself. "I go," he said numbly. "I go."

What Olaf said then brought them both to their senses. "Pa, don't you think it's time we began to act like grown men? I guess we both have to stop this running away."

"All right, tie us up again," Leander conceded reluctantly. He sat on a net box, breathing heavily. It had been a close call; He'd almost shown Olaf the man nobody knew and, God willing, no one ever would.

The wind fell during the night—by morning, there was barely enough breeze to sail by.

Cruising out toward their wind-stressed nets at seven o'clock, Leander pointed and said to Olaf, "That Nels Martinson from Chambers Island, he's out by his nets already. I wish we could see from here if he found them; if his are there, ours will be too."

Riding smoothly on the calmest sea they could hope for in December, Leander sat on a net box and contemplated the vagaries of a fisherman's life. A lakes fisherman daily swung like a pendulum between despair and elation, from the extreme of fear to pure relief. Meantime he grew a wry neck from gazing at the sky. A wind that lulled a landlubber to sleep kept a fisherman's wife walking the floor.

"If that breeze doesn't pick up, it'll take us a while yet to get out there; I think I could row us faster." Leander was standing now, leaning against the centerboard rack as he spoke to Olaf at the tiller. "But I'm glad the wind went down. It helps my toothache."

Gliding slowly across the water to the gang of nets set a mile from shore, he gestured starboard. "That Arvidson, he beat us out there too," he commented and stepped to the bow. Arvid Arvidson and his boys had come up from Green Bay to take in the fall herring run. They camped in a rude lean-to on the next brook down shore.

Out of the blue, a premonition prickled over Leander and he turned to Olaf standing in the stern. "Olaf!" he cried. Olaf, only a boatlength away, was being swallowed up by a writhing, white mass of fog.

Olaf answered, "Well, Pa, I guess we're swamped in now," but his voice, though clear, seemed to come from nowhere.

Now when the wind shall blow: Leander brooded to himself, it probably will not, maybe for two days or more. He flailed at the fog breathlessly for the dense, obscuring mist seemed to shut off his air; it was like being sewn inside a goosedown pillow.

"We've lost sight of Aaron and Stephan in the *Flicka*!" he said in alarm. "They were close behind us."

"We better take in sail and come around and head for

shore,'' Olaf proposed. "We'll have to row, there's almost no wind at all now.''

Leander felt his way astern, but it was like swimming in the womb. A voice hailed. From starboard? Yes, it was Arvidson. Then there was a crack of gunwales close under his hand and, reaching, he touched the hull of the Arvidson's pound boat, the *Anna Petra*.

"We have to head for shore or we lose our direction,'' Arvidson said in Swedish. Then in English, "What do you think?''

Before Leander could answer, there was another voice hallooing in the fog. "Hello, Hello! Can anybody hear us? We are Martinsons from the Island.''

"Johannsens, here,'' Olaf shouted back through cupped hands.

The voice came again, "We are mixed up already. We go ashore with you?''

"Arvidson is here too,'' Olaf yelled, "but we have to turn around. We should come ashore if we do that. We can use a sounding line.''

Within a few minutes, still other voices were heard in the strange acoustics of the whiteout: Aaron's and Stephan's were among them, but where were they? With much calling, it seemed the boats were headed in some sort of flotilla toward the Michigan shore; then one by one the voices began to fade and Leander knew he and Olaf were alone, drifting, he was convinced, right out the Door of Death into the big lake.

Sculling shoreward (or were they really headed that way?), noises of beaten pan and bell could be heard faintly and, off somewhere a foghorn and shouting, but where? Unnerved, in a spasm of near hysteria, he groped his way to the stern, wrested the oar from Olaf and sent the craft to port.

"No, no!'' Olaf was upset, there was nothing wrong with his voice now. "You're taking us off course!''

"I hear Helga, I go to her right now,'' Leander insisted. "A scare would be the worst thing for her.''

"Well you won't find Ma that way,'' Olaf threw out the words, flying in the face of his father. "You've got us headed for Menominee or maybe Sturgeon Bay. Give the oar back to me.''

"You take us out the Door!'' Leander objected, consternation rising in his voice. "We'll be lost!''

"Pa, this fog won't last forever—the weather'll move

through. I'll scull us slowly ashore. I know that's what Aaron is doing."

Then Leander gathered his wits enough to say what he thought they must do. "Then we'll drop anchor and stay right here."

"No! It's only half a mile to shore."

Why did Olaf have to be so stubborn? Leander fumbled his way to the bow, found the anchor and heaved it overboard in a burst of frustration and anger. Satisfied with himself, he leaned on the gunwale and felt automatically if the hook had caught; but there was no tension on the rope, nothing in his hand but a loose length of anchor line.

Now he'd done it! Of all the stupid fits of temper he'd had in his life, this was the most dangerous. They would drift now at the mercy of the current unless they rowed steadily. They would go out the Door or smash on island or shoal when night came if they weren't beached somewhere by then. A wind would surely come up as the fog lifted, which would most likely be after dark, and blow them where it pleased. Almost certainly, a freezing rain would begin to fall; with a wild December wind, that would do it.

He'd told Helga on many stormy nights, "A wind like this will call my name one day."

She'd always laughed and said, "Leander, you'll die in bed like the rest of us."

He'd never bought himself a watch, having always set his inner timepiece by the sun, but now he needed something more reliable. When he judged it to be ten o'clock in the morning, he asked Olaf, "You got the time?"

"I lost my watch three months ago," Olaf responded, dead voiced.

Too late, Leander remembered Olaf had thrown his thick pocket watch into the grave with Mandy's coffin. "I'll row awhile," he said then, lamely striving to keep Olaf from withdrawing into silence again.

"You'd better let me," Olaf said. His tone indicated that he was clamming up but he went on, "With one oar, you'll row us in a circle with nothing to navigate by. Give it to me."

As Olaf's last words trailed off, Leander bitterly regretted having mentioned the time of day. But how would they know when to eat their noon meal of bread and coffee? Time was standing still. He was hungry now.

Olaf would soon tire of sculling the wide-beamed, heavy boat into sea mist so dense you could only dimly see your hand in front of your face in daylight. By now, neither of them had any idea of their location, only that they were blind and anchorless on a perfectly flat sea. Any minute now they might go aground on the rocky west shore of the long island or grind onto the gravelly underwater ridge that was Whaleback Shoal.

The fog seemed to settle then, to become more gray and static. Several times Leander thought he heard his own fog horn, probably being blown by Garnet; but when they tried to proceed toward it, the sound faded away.

After a time (how many hours?), he told Olaf, "My tooth still hurts, it feels like somebody's driving a nail in my jaw. I think I'll lay down in the bottom of the boat a little bit."

Olaf's only answer was a grunt of assent.

When Leander awakened, the world was as dark as the inside of a stoppered jug, but a fresh cold wind was tossing the boat. With an ascending scream, he sat up from the floor of the craft. "Olaf? Olaf, *Olaf*!" No answer. He groped about the boat on both sides of the centerboard and mast from stern to bow. "Olaf, answer me," he pleaded in the Norwegian of his childhood. "Olaf!"

Olaf was not aboard!

He slid to the fishy-smelling floor planks of the boat again, raking his back on the projecting corner handle of a fish box. Suddenly he remembered telling Helga after the horrible incident in the flower garden in June, "I'll be dead, but they'll not bury me." One day, some fisherman would come across the *Guld* locked in the ice, his frozen body aboard. It was not his fate to be quickly drowned in a tempest, he knew that now. He would die of toothache and starvation and bitter cold. Why? Why in God's name had Olaf sought his own death, leaving his father to die by inches? At this terminal point in his despair, morning with rescue did not occur to him.

He sat there in the narrow aisle between the stacks of fish boxes, his feet straight out before him, his head drooping. In his imagination, he'd been sitting there interminably, hungry, cold and cringing from the pain shooting from his eyetooth to his brain.

A bump, a knee between his shoulder blades and a hand brushing off his cap brought him to himself.

"Olaf? Oh, Olaf," he sobbed unmanfully.

"Pa, I've been trying to find you. We've been going around the boat behind each other in this black."

Abruptly, Leander was furious at his son. He stood up and swung about to swipe at Olaf. "Boy, why don't you answer when I talk to you?"

In the pitchy dark, the open boat rose and fell and the wind increased in velocity and chill until a few rifts of light appeared in the black sky.

"We'd better pray that's a northeast wind," Leander said to himself for Olaf wasn't talking. It should have been morning, but it wasn't, when Leander felt the first drops of precipitation. It was rain, a freezing rain, the last thing they needed.

He groped and found Olaf sitting on the floor in the stern. "We'll lay on the bottom of the boat and pull the tarp over us," he told his son gently.

How many hours later was it when they felt the blessed drag of sand on the *Guld's* flat bottom, then a jolting smack? They pried back the frozen tarp and looked out for signs of dawn. It was there! Astern in the rain! They were on the mainland of Michigan.

"Pa," Olaf began and there was even a hint of rejoicing in his voice, "Pa, I think there's enough light for us to find the last piece of bread and eat it."

Huddled in their frozen canvas cave, they ate. The *Guld* was wedged against a large boulder but there was no hole in her.

Dim daybreak came, and scanning the shore, Leander whooped. He'd seen it plain, the mouth of Mathias Bailey's creek. "We'll find a pole!" he exulted. "We'll pry this boat off that rock and go home to Mama for coffee."

20

A Sepulcher of Ice

It was not yet daylight on Christmas morning when Aaron rose from the wooden couch where he'd spent the night in the big kitchen of his parent's cottage. The house was cold and there was no sound except the whickering, wornout snores of his father and Stephan. He pulled up the suspenders of his pants and dressed his feet for the outdoors. Then he knew the import of the silence in the rest of the cabin—it was all over.

Reluctant, yet driven, he turned up the wall lamp by the cookstove and entered the chamber where Garnet had been sitting up with their mother since midnight. Inside, he stared, rubbing the sleep from his eyes. There was no one in the room. It was empty! Then he saw by the turned-down lamp on the dresser that there were two faint mounds under the white spread covering the thick feather bed and two capped figures surrounded by pillows arranged to hold back the encroaching cold.

He stood there, holding himself, letting shock, relief and sorrow flow over him by turns. There was no hurry now. At first he thought he'd go to his house and get Liza, then he told himself, Aaron, you're a big boy now. Just take it easy and do what has to be done.

At his touch on her shoulder, Garnet sat up instantly and loosed her hand with difficulty from that of his mother's. "Mr. Aaron, oh, Mr. Aaron!" she mourned. "I hain't been sleepin'?"

"Yes, thank God," he consoled her and added; "but there's something you must do before my father hears us."

Garnet pushed back the gather cap she'd donned at the first chill of nightfall, turned to the form beside her in the bed and saw

115

what he meant. "Oh, Lord God," she lamented, her voice rising shrilly, "I done fall asleep when Miss Helga need me."

"Don't worry, Aunt Garnet, she just slipped away or you'd have heard her. Nobody could have done more for Ma than you did."

While he stood there, Garnet laid back the covers and emerging fully clothed, walked around the fourposter bed, closed his mother's eyes, smoothed the contours of her face and folded the bone-thin hands. Last of all, she crossed the indigo shawl from Tennessee about the child-sized shoulders and pulled up the spread.

Aaron returned to the couch in the front room to sit quietly a moment, head between his knees, fortifying himself before he must awaken his father. Pondering a procedure for the next hours, he was comforted by the existence of a good sleigh road to the cemetery at Cedar Forks. Then his mind was offended by the thought of Olaf returning with their mother to the very spot on Spalding's tote road where Mandy lay under the snow and frozen earth.

Who would help him dig the grave under the worst of winter conditions? Not Olaf, nor Bjorn, who'd quit his job with Gunnar and was home again, waiting for the bay to make ice enough to set the winter gill nets. August Greutzmacher would do it, and he was thankful for the German who fitted so agreeably into their family.

Keening softly to herself, Garnet came out of the bedroom and began to build a fire in the cookstove. Aaron jumped up to lay dry wood on the coals in the box heater and went into the other bedroom to awaken his father and granduncle.

Without looking at the covered form on the bed, their father had reached behind his bedroom door, taken his black wedding suit from a peg on the wall and gone back into the spare room to dress. So far, he'd not spoken to anyone.

Aaron looked around the now warm kitchen where the clan was gathered. Bjorn was beginning to fidget with hunger and his own stomach complained. Their father sat in a straight chair, guarding the door that had been shut on their mother's body. Finally Aaron asked, "Liza could you boil us a pot of coffee and bake a pan of biscuits?"

As Garnet crossed the room to help Liza, their father rose

from his chair, a faint mask of mania on his face, and declared, "We do not eat today."

"But Pa," Aaron argued gently, "That's not what Ma would want at all. It's Christmas Day, and no matter how badly we feel, we have to act like it's Christmas for her sake."

Their father laid a protecting hand on the sliding wood latch of the door. "If you want to make merry, get out of here," he told them, his voice unrecognizable with grief. "Do your celebrating somewhere else and leave us alone."

Naomi looked up in bewilderment at her mother, and the others in the room kept their gazes on the floor in uncertainty and embarrassment.

While the room was in this momentary limbo, Tippy slipped through to the guarded door and began to scratch at it vigorously. Their father upended the dog with a thrust of his boot, but the terrier came back and made one eery, wavering howl before he laid down at his master's feet with his nose on his paws.

It came to Aaron then: Ma has done what we all must do in the end. Now we must finish the part for her that she cannot do.

He stepped to the middle of the room, taking charge as was his duty if Olaf could not. "Liza," he began again, "Maybe you'd better go to our house and fix us all some breakfast."

"Bjorn," he continued, "you can help Olaf do the barn chores while Uncle Stephan and August go to the woodshed and fetch what they've made."

Garnet got up then and spoke hesitantly, "I got to do what Miss Helga tell me," and moved toward the closed door.

Their father made a menacing gesture, ordering her to sit down again. "You can't go in there now."

"I got to. I promise Miss Helga I git it fer little Naomi de fust thing on Christmas mornin'."

With rage flaring on his face, their father clung to the closed door, preventing her, then he looked about at the shocked faces of his family and dropped his hand.

In the bedroom only a moment, Garnet emerged with a porcelain-headed doll dressed in scraps of their mother's blue velvet wedding gown. "Your Grandma make dis fer you last summer," she explained, holding out the doll to the little girl.

Their father was tensing for a lunge at the doll and Aaron cried, "Pa! Remember Ma's flowers!"

Sagging and choking back dry sobs, the grieving man gave

leave for them to do what they must with a small wave of his hand, went into the spare room and shut the door.

With his exit, the room came alive. Naomi began to chatter, "I got to tell Grandma Johannsen, 'Thank you.' I want her to think of a name for my dolly."

"Ye cain't," Garnet said bluntly.

"Why?"

"She gone to visit Miss Mandy."

The child ran to the window facing the breaking dawn. "I don't see any new stars."

"Ye will. Tonight, I'll show ye."

Eating breakfast in his own house, Aaron recalled that, when they were children, their mother had taken pains to tell them about death. When the spark of life went out, she believed, the body became an empty husk to be disposed of as quickly and reverently as possible. Now death had come to her and they must proceed to carry out her belief. To do so, meant they must nourish themselves; and she'd have approved of Liza's high and crusty biscuits, wild strawberry sun-preserves and bacon and eggs.

Things would have seemed almost as usual, had not their father felt obliged to stay in his cabin by the closed door behind which the coffin stood on sawhorses. Could he not sense their mother's new capability to be with him there in his lonely chair and also with the family at the morning meal? Her presence was as much a reality in Liza's kitchen as the aroma of freshly ground coffee.

They were resting quietly for a moment after finishing the food when their father came in the door and stood just inside, blowing from the cold. "Boys," he directed peremptorily, "take the ice saw and go out and cut blocks of ice out of the *Guld's* slip. Stephan, you help Garnet take care of Mama. August can help me find timbers to make a curb for the box."

"Pa," their father was out of his mind and Aaron began to reason cautiously with him, "Pa, wait, we got to go to the cemetery and dig a grave, at least I have to."

Olaf spoke from compounded sorrow, his pleasant face had aged until he seemed almost as old as their father, "I'll help you, Aaron. I recall what you and Bjorn did for Mandy."

Aaron's heart ached for his brother and he remembered Henning who had also been gentle like their mother. Henning could have comforted Olaf now, as the rest could not.

"No!" their father was shrilly insisting, "We'll pack the box in ice blocks behind the woodshed. I promised Mama I'd take her back to Ephraim in the spring."

"Pa, you can't do that!" his sons protested in unison.

"I can. I must do it."

"You'll only make it hard for yourself and the rest of us."

"I keep my promise."

Aaron came close to blurting, "Pa, Ma's not in that box, she never will be. She'll be here, walking and talking with us and playing with Liza's new baby." Baby! they'd forgotten about Annie who now had two babies; they must get word to her somehow.

Then he observed again the thin, stooped, but still forceful figure of their father, standing there, ignoring Liza's invitation to eat. "Pa," he coaxed, "you eat some breakfast, and we'll do what you say. I never thought of it, but I see your point now. Don't you?" he turned to the boys, seeking confirmation.

"I wanted Ma to lie beside Mandy, almost holding hands," Olaf said, "but I remember how she loved Ephraim. Pa's right. We must take her across the bay in the spring."

"I'll take her white piney, that yellow rose and the blue flag plants in the boat with her," their father said and left the house without eating.

Working, chopping ice at ten o'clock, Aaron could hear a whinny that could only belong to the Nicholsons' amiable Sam. It was things like that reinforced your belief in God. Who else could have sent Dorcas, Carl and Gunnar when they were needed on a bitterly cold Christmas morning? An answer to an unsaid prayer, they slid into the clearing on the seat of a clumsy freighting sleigh, and he walked up the path to greet them.

"Merry Christmas," Dorcas called, but her voice trailed off; she'd seen his face. When the vehicle halted, she asked simply, "Your mother?"

"Yes, this morning. We're getting ready to do for her. Could you help Garnet when you get warmed up?"

"Garnet laid out our Mandy so pretty. I'll do the best I can."

By mid-afternoon, the cairn of ice had been completed over the pine box and they all stood in the blustery cold of a waning winter day while Carl Nicholson found his place in the Swedish Bible. Aaron took one of their father's hands and Olaf, the other, and the older man did not resist. Their moves started a chain of reaction until all those standing about the improvised grave were holding hands. Eyes were dry, it was too cold and sad for tears.

"The Lord is my shepherd," Carl Nicholson read in Swedish, and Aaron could hear Garnet repeating the foreign words their mother had taught her. It would have been nice to hear the cherished organ, but music would come in the spring at the Moravian Church in Ephraim.

When the speaker had finished, "and I shall dwell in the house of the Lord forever," they slowly led their father back to the house. It was time for him to eat.

Walking around the sagging net fence of their mother's snowy garden, Naomi kept scanning the sky and tugging at Garnet. "Don't forget, you promised me you'd show me Grandma Johannsen's star tonight."

Listening to the child, walking with an arm about Liza's ballooning figure, Aaron shivered, struck with a chill beyond the weather. What's the matter with me? he asked himself. The first thing I know I'll be as spooky as Garnet concerning the future.

21

Death Floe

A strong breeze like the breath of doom came up by two o'clock; even on a bright February day when earth and water were frozen, fishermen were not safe from the wind. Liza felt irresistibly drawn to the window facing the bay, and Garnet fussed at her, "Come away from thar; ye cain't do a thing 'bout dat blowin'."

"I think I'll go to the coopershop and talk to Olaf."

"Hain't no use. He standin' on de dock with his spyglass up to his eye."

Emotions raced through Liza, tumbling too fast to be sorted, but fear, disappointment and frustration were among them. "I'm afraid," she went on. "Olaf told Aaron the ice was rotten out there."

"Hit hain't natural, men walkin' on de water."

"Aaron told Olaf, 'It's safe as the floor in your house, if the wind doesn't blow too hard'."

"I tell you what Stephan say, 'Ifen hit do blow, hit's a widow-maker. He say hit take de men and horses right out dat place he call de Door of Death'."

Liza continued to gaze out at the twenty-mile-wide frozen bay extending like a prairie to the dark finger of the Wisconsin peninsula. It was hard to believe that a single strong gust of wind could break the plain of ice into death floes. Then she remembered the jokes the men had told about so-and-so's good crack-jumping horses, but no one had said whether Buck and Kate had that talent.

Back in Tennessee, she'd not be standing at a window, praying for God to stop a wind not yet strong enough to lift a shingle on the roof, but here such a gale was capable of leaving her and hers homelsss and destitute. If Stephan, Aaron, Leander and Bjorn were blown out the Door, what would she, Naomi, Garnet and the baby do? She would have to squelch her fear of the water and go on the bay like a man and get food for her family. Olaf could in no way be expected to take on Aaron's and Stephan's responsibilities.

Olaf was staying now at his vantage point on the dock. What did he see? Whatever it was, it was not good. Liza bundled herself in Aaron's warm coat and made her way to the sunny, cold and windswept dock. There she stood with her back to the wind, inquiring mutely of Olaf. When he gave no comment, she ventured, "Olaf, I know you're worried. Do you reckon I could look through that glass for a minute and see for myself?"

"You can look, but you'll see nothing." He handed her the telescope.

Panic, then terror surged; Olaf's tone said the ice had already broken off. She steadied herself against a post and peered through the glass; there were still gill netters scattered about on the ice. What did Olaf mean? "Can you be sure you don't see the Johannsens?" she asked.

"There's nothing but blue water where Buck and Kate were a few minutes ago. Don't you think you'd better go in the house? If they're lost, other fishermen will come and tell us soon enough."

How could she go anywhere when her legs were filled with sand and could not be trusted to hold up the load she was carrying? Olaf followed her into the house and made her sit on a chair while he poured her a cup of tea. Her heart failed when she thought of the good husband he'd have made for Mandy.

Olaf moved his tea cup in a design on the table top. "Liza," he said forthrightly, "I have to tell you, I'm scared. That's what I don't like about commercial fishing on this treacherous bay; the men always feel obliged to take risks; it's a failing they're born with, I guess."

And she was just the one who'd soon bear another fisherman who'd grow up to make his living on the bay.

Olaf left his tea and went out to the Johannsens' pile of firewood poles and began to chop the everlastingly needed stove blocks. Even though the Johannsens had bunked together in the two houses north of the brook since Helga's death, with four stoves to feed instead of six, Garnet now spent most of her day chopping, carrying and stoking the green wood. Aaron promised the inestimable benefit of dry wood another winter; in cold weather, you could never quite get a house warm with fresh cut trees.

Liza was drawn again to the window overlooking the fishing fields, and the shocking prospect of never seeing Aaron again wrung her body like birthing pains and she feared for the baby; a winter infant just had to be full term. The spasms eased; she sat down, but she had to brace herself to keep her body from oozing off the chair.

In the months she'd been a fisherman's wife, the scares had come with dismaying regularity, including the time Leander and Olaf had been out all night in the fog. Sometimes it was hard to tell if the Johannsen men were courageous or foolhardy, but Aaron had told her, "A man has to stay off the water if he doesn't want to take chances; that's how we make a living. Of course we're scared—a man who isn't afraid when he's in danger won't last long."

"Uncle Stephan says there's fine land for new farms only a few miles west and south of here," she'd said doggedly, willfully steering the conversation in a direction he despised.

"Have you thought about how you can safely cut down eighty acres of big maple trees so they can rot and make way for your crops?" Aaron had shot back. "In a new land, you're in danger just sitting in your cabin; a peddler can come by and give you smallpox."

Olaf came in the house with an armload of wood and stood, stony-faced as he had been for months after Mandy's death, staring out the window. Garnet, starting supper for the crew, seemed not to realize Stephan was with the missing men.

To moderate her terror, Liza got up and went to the dry sink to peel potatoes for Garnet. Through the pane above, she could see distant black specks moving ashore. In an hour the bay would be cleared of all gill netters and the Johannsen men would be home or the terrible vigil would continue. Naomi hung by Olaf, pestering him to hear her reading lesson. "I think it's time we went to the shop to see how August is doing," he suggested to the little girl at last. "Get your coat and gaiters on."

Liza watched them walk past Helga's house and up the brook past the woodshed near where Helga's body lay in its grave of ice. "Oh, Mama Johannsen," she cried wordlessly, "If you could only tell us if the men be with you."

Then without bidding, the lifelike image of Norris Peake

came to her and she could feel his arms again, comforting her. She blindly cut a potato in quarters and peeled the pieces. How could a woman need and feel the arms of two men?

The baby's protesting somersault brought her mind back to its father and the gripping hope that Aaron had somehow escaped when the ice broke off. But hope dwindled to gall when darkness fell, the wind laid and the cold descended. Except for Naomi's plate, Garnet's supper sat warming on the back of the stove. The wrinkled old woman had been in the bedroom for several minutes and Liza knew without investigating that she was in a trance of prayer. Olaf's face was like granite, and August Greutzmacher could not hold back the tears. It would be a long night.

She'd been listening so intently for a sound; still, the blowing of a horse startled her. She flung open the door and a strange horse and rider stood at the step. The animal was white, and for a fleeting moment she associated the pair with the Pale Horse and Rider Aaron had spoken of.

"I'm your neighbor Nelson, up the shore," the man in the shadows said. "I've come to tell you that your men have been sighted on the shove ice on Whaleback Shoal."

"The horses?" Olaf was at the door.

"No horses, no equipment."

"There's no way to get our men off the reef?" Olaf pressed.

"Not tonight. But the wind's gone down; some of the ice'll drift back and freeze in this cold."

"The men'll freeze."

"Not if they didn't get wet."

"What can we do?"

"If you're praying people, as I've heard you are, you can pray ."

Liza began to do as the man said, then she thought of Garnet. In her relief and excitement, she reverted to mountain talk as she opened the door where the older woman lay face down on the bed in the chilling room. "Git up, Garnet," she urged, "hit be hall right. Uncle Stephan and the rest be on a rock."

Garnet sat up, cross-legged in the middle of the puffy bed, put her palms together in an attitude of prayer and promised, "Dear Lord God, I goin' to do anything Ye say from now on. I hain't goin' to have no bad thoughts 'bout ary people."

How long is a night? A quick passage of time for lovers, a short hour of rest for the weary, an eternity of waiting for lost loved ones. But morning ever comes and it did. At daybreak, Liza watched Olaf and August proceed toward the shoal, across the solid ice, with a group of men with hand sleighs and a small boat.

When the sun was high enough to light the area where the men must be, she, Naomi and Garnet went out in the below zero cold and stood with the telescope on the snowy dock. Garnet scanned the bay then said, "Ifen ye give me de glass, I git me a ladder and go up on de shop roof where I cain see better."

Liza waited with Naomi while Garnet perched on her improvised widow's walk and she remembered telling Aaron's mother, "There's nary a place a woman don't set and wait."

Garnet swung the glass, focusing, searching. She put it down to rest her good eye and looked again. "Oh, Miss Liza!" she shouted finally, "dey do be specks on dat ice ridge!"

"Oh, Garnet, be sure, count them."

"I did, dey be four and dey be men."

22

Simon Peter

The sky was a gray feather bed threatening to descend intact upon the earth when Aaron left with the sleigh and the new team of horses to get Mrs. Strauss. He was barely able to control the dappled grays in the frosty weather and Liza recalled Leander's remark of the previous winter, "Some feller bought Illinois horses cheap." Well her father-in-law had fallen into the same mire after Buck and Kate had been lost. The new animals were not yet four years old and Liza knew Aaron and the men risked their lives each time they went out to lift gill nets with them.

After Aaron had departed to Sam Hayward's stage station to pick up the German midwife from Marinette, Liza thought about the woman she'd never seen. Was she the kind of midwife who'd hold your hand when the pains were unbearable or would she turn her back, preferring not to face agony till she had to? Liza couldn't help resenting Aaron's interference; Garnet would have been enough; the slave woman had brought Naomi into the world.

"But it doesn't matter who's with me," she said to herself. "In the end, Simon Peter and I'll have to give him life by ourselves."

Garnet had been sleeping with Stephan in Naomi's room since Helga's death at Christmas. She'd not take kindly to being moved out so a strange woman could take care of her own. Liza let her hand drop to her abdomen and remarked to Garnet, "They can talk all they want, *this* is the way you get commercial fishermen; it may be a man's world and a man's work, but a woman sets the boat asail."

Garnet was morose about giving up her room to Mrs. Strauss.

"I be de one should stay close by and do for you," she muttered. "Dat woman don't know how to fotch a bunch of cats."

"I have to do what Aaron thinks is best; he's upset and worried."

When Liza saw Eva Strauss, she concurred with Garnet. The gaunt, green-eyed woman wore her hair in a spiraling knot on top of her head which made her seem taller and even more commanding. She came in the door with Aaron and commented after introductions, "Vell, vell, it looks like ve got efryt'ing ve neet here. Vich is my room? I rest a v'ile."

"I cain tell when I'm not wanted," Garnet proclaimed audibly and left, carrying her personal belongings in a bundle to Leander's house where she and Stephan would sleep in Helga's bed again. "Hain't no sense in hall dis movin' 'round for no foreign woman," she said clearly as she slammed the door.

Garnet was partly right and Aaron was beginning to see it. They were all dismayed and concerned about the midwife's sniffly, runny cold; and the next morning, Mrs. Strauss was in bed with a fever and the grippe.

Now Liza could see that Aaron was really uneasy. "I guess too much has happened, I must not be thinking straight," he apologized. "Liza, I should have let well enough alone when you insisted Garnet could do for you. She'd going to do it anyway, by the look of things."

"You did what you thought was right. It's too late now, backward looking don't help."

"I've got a good notion to take Mrs. Strauss back to Marinette."

"You can't, she's a sick woman; besides, I have her cold already."

Wiping the supper dishes for Liza, Aaron looked out at the evening sky. "I guess we're stuck with the situation as it is," he said then; "and that's not all, before another night we'll get our March blizzard."

"Don't worry, between Garnet and Mrs. Strauss, they have every medicine there is."

By morning it had come, not a blizzard, but a silently laid foot of snow and more coming; the great feather bed of precipitation had split. Liza was standing by the window watching the ghostly men trying to keep up with the thickly falling snow with wooden shovels when she felt the first twinge. Mrs. Strauss coughed ceaselessly and was down in bed, requiring nursing care. Who would look after the midwife now?

Liza walked the floor at intervals all day with a sore throat adding to her discomfort, and the snow fell steadily. The weather was so warm, only the cookstove fire was needed. After supper her pains bore down and she said to Aaron, "Now I think we can get down to the business of having us a baby."

When irresistible contractions put her on her knees by the couch, Aaron came in from emptying Mrs. Strauss's slopjar and said, "This is enough. I'm going to fetch Garnet, she's sulked in her cabin too long now."

By morning there was a respite from the snow, but there was a promise of more in the opaque gray sky. Except for Aaron, the men shoveled snow all day. By nightfall, Aaron was ready to go for Dorcas Nicholson, and Liza couldn't wait for him to go. Garnet, hovering now, insisted over and over again, "A youngun got to be born in one night and one day from de fust pain or dere be trouble brewin'."

Simon Peter was a big one and reluctant to make his appearance into a hostile world of ice and cold and kegged fish. Liza began to cough a duet with Mrs. Strauss and her throat was painfully raw. She barely had time to watch Aaron drive off with the rambunctious new horses to get Dorcas Nicholson when a contraction forced her on a nearby chair and a scream took her unawares.

Garnet came from the cookstove and started a solicitous keening. For the first time, Liza told her, "Shut up, help me get undressed and in my bed."

The German woman came to her door, coughing wrackingly and wheezing for breath. "Mrs. Eckberg," she directed, "You got to get Mrs. Johannsen sitting on a pail of real warm water. Can you turn the baby? If it don't come soon, it's butt first."

Garnet gave her a scathing look and muttered, "You go set on a bucket of hot water yoreself."

In the bed, catching a few blessed breaths between pains, Liza felt milk surge into her breasts and begin to drip on the front of her nightgown. Was that what was causing the tightness in her chest?

The coughing started again, pressing the baby harder against her pelvis. He would be suffocated. When the paroxysm was over, she lay, limp as a rag on her pillow; then after an hour of regular pains, she sat up again, gasping for air. She could barely breathe.

A tearing contraction took her again and she could get no air into her lungs. She was going to die.

The night was mild and Aaron opened the window; there were too many people in the room, using up Liza's breath of life. Garnet was practicing all the lore she knew to ease Liza's pneumonia while he and Dorcas were doing little but wait for the baby to be born. In spite of Eva Strauss's grim prediction that the baby might present himself bottom first, the infant's black hair had been showing.

The bed was low and Aaron's back was breaking from stooping over Liza so she could grasp his hands with bruising force. He knew his own pain was sympathetic, his sinewy back was used to bending all day, pulling fish-laden nets up through holes in the ice. It was terror tightening his muscles; Liza's slim body could not long endure the often simultaneous seizures of coughing and labor contractions. He excused himself to Dorcas, went out in the fresh night air and dropped on the porch step. The moonlight glimmered on his mother's resting place. "Ma," he appealed aloud, "oh, Ma, help us."

After a moment, he got control of himself and returned to the kitchen where Olaf lingered anxiously by the confinement room door and their father paced from cookstove to heater, firing each to excess so the outside door had to be kept open. August Greutzmacher was in the widow Strauss's room, comforting her and doing what he could for her lighter case of pneumonia. Stephan and Bjorn were caring for Naomi in his father's cabin.

Aaron fought off a tempting fainting reaction when he reentered the sick room and Dorcas turned back the sheet covering Liza. The tall woman drew above the perineum with her finger. "Aaron, we'll have to cut here or she'll be torn to pieces."

He clung to the carved pine post of the bed. "What'll we use?" he managed to ask.

"Your razor, I think; tell Olaf to boil it."

Garnet had rigged a bed sheet tent above the upper half of Liza's body with a kettle full of steaming infusion under it. Her brown face steamed with sweat as she repeatedly checked the thin mustard plasters on the top front and back of Liza's chest. Between times, she spooned a bitter smelling liquid in Liza's mouth and rubbed her arms and hands when they were not clutching in terrible labor.

Staying available to help Dorcas at the foot of the bed, it

struck Aaron that the intervals between Liza's pains were lengthening and their intensity was lessening. The baby would have to be born soon or never. Now he knew why it was said his Uncle Edward Aaronson had slept in a separate room from his wife after their only child, the giant Eino, had been born.

Olaf brought the razor to Dorcas, and turning to Liza, she directed over her shoulder, "Olaf, hold both lamps."

Aaron held his wife's legs, but Dorcas delayed. "She's pushing! Cut!" he cried.

Dorcas made a timid slash, then another. Liza bore down with a long shriek and a large baby's head appeared. Now the shoulders; Aaron forgot himself and shouted hoarsely, "Push, Liza, push!" though she did not hear him.

"Press like this on her abdomen," Dorcas showed him. "I'll pull."

How could he do that when Dorcas was going to hurt his wife and baby? He felt himself wavering toward the floor, the good solid boards. "Olaf, Olaf!" he wept, looking wildly at his brother. But Olaf was oblivious and obsessed, willing the baby to be born.

"Now!" Dorcas begged, her voice shrill.

Then a bloody baby boy lay on the delivery pad but he was dead. No! Dorcas was telling Olaf, her tone sharp under stress. "Get the pans of warm and cool water."

Olaf set the lamps on the dresser and did as he'd been instructed earlier in the evening, and together he and Dorcas slapped and dunked the baby. When the blue infant began to whimper and flush, Olaf hugged the slippery body to his woolen shirt then handed him to Dorcas.

"Find me a chair," Aaron told Olaf then, for the room was pitching like the *Liten Flicka* in a wild blow and his sea legs were limp.

But Liza moaned his name under the pneumonia tent and he made himself rise to the stature of a new father. Garnet laid back the sheet tent so he could hold his wife and brush back her dark hair.

"Liza, you did good," he told his fever-warm wife. "Simon Peter's here."

Suddenly Dorcas cried out in unbelieving shock, "My God! she's bleeding!"

Olaf rolled the baby in the blanket Dorcas thrust at him. "Give the baby to Leander!" she told him frantically. "You and Aaron must help me!"

Through the thin board partition between the bedrooms, Eva Strauss had heard the portent in Dorcas's exclamation—hemorrhage, and she stood in the door, wheezing in her nightdress. "You must let me try to stop the bleeding," she said, hanging to August and the door jamb.

Dorcas raised her head from the pack she was desperately applying. "Have you done it before? Oh, if you can, please do it. I've never seen such a thing."

Heedless of exposing herself, the German woman pulled up the long skirt of her nightgown and knelt on the bed, facing Liza's feet, and grasped Liza's lower abdomen in both hands. She held on, kneading, while Aaron supported her and Dorcas hurriedly dressed the baby. When the midwife could no longer send strength to her weakened arms and hands, Dorcas took her place and Aaron monitored the packs. Olaf had returned to the kitchen with the baby.

Their father was holding the lamp now. The bleeding had dwindled by the grace of God, and now it seemed important to spare Garnet who, by the blue pallor of her skin, was at the point of falling on her face. "Olaf," Aaron called, "Lay the baby in his box and come take Garnet's place."

Olaf was a natural nurse. He and his dead sweetheart's mother remained in vigilance in Liza's room while Aaron went to fetch Stephan and made a fresh pot of coffee. It was two o'clock in the morning.

Abruptly, August put down his coffee cup and left the house like a man bent on an urgent errand. He returned with a cunningly fashioned cradle made from barrel staves and half headings. Dorcas came out and laid the baby in it. Simon Peter, wide awake now, seemed to smile when Aaron rocked the cradle gently. "You little booger, you blessed little booger," he choked.

The nervous tension began to drain away, then Liza restarted the wracking coughing. Aaron got up to go to her, but he felt himself falling and saw sparks when his head hit the floor. How long had he lain there, stretched straight out? His father and Stephan were attempting to raise him. There was a painful goose egg on the back of his head. He sat up, shaking off the half-crying old men who were trying to aid him. He'd never fainted during the whole hideous war; it was a shame his family had to see him pass out like a woman now.

He staggered to his feet and went in the bedroom. Liza had her eyes closed and she was fighting for every breath. He earnestly prayed then that there'd be no more coughing. Then he saw the wet stain on the bosom of her nightgown and he knew with stunning insight that the turning point of their tribulation had not been reached. *How could they feed Simon Peter if Liza remained so ill?* The cow was dry as most others were in winter. Like newborn calves and pigs, the baby must have at least a few ounces of new milk; there was something about it that insured health.

"Even if Liza can nurse the baby, he'll catch her sickness, won't he?" Aaron asked Dorcas anxiously.

"I've heard that young ones are protected from such things for five or six weeks, " she sought to reassure him.

"Don't you think we should try to get some milk into Simon Peter now?" He couldn't say, "In case Liza dies."

"By noon," Dorcas agreed.

Simon Peter had one good stomach full then there was no more milk. At supper, Garnet spooned sugar water into the hungry infant, but soon he began a ceaseless wailing. In confusion, Aaron delved into his mind. How could a man feed his newborn son? What folk tale had he heard a long time ago, that men and old women could be stimulated to give milk for orphan infants?

Dorcas broke in on his thoughts, "You know, Aaron, we have to find a wetnurse the first thing in the morning."

"Where? Do you know anyone with a new baby in Cedar Forks?"

"I know of three women, a prostitute full of sores, a Mrs. McCord who has eleven children and Mrs. No-Sah-We-Quet."

"Wood Fern, Mrs. Jacob No-Sah-We-Quet? They were here several times last summer with berries and maple sugar."

"She's your best prospect."

The atmosphere of the calm pre-dawn was like April as Aaron drove the obstreperous team out the swamp road with the sleigh loaded with baled hay for the No-Sah-We-Quet's two scrawny ponies. (Alec and Jacob had piled lumber for Spalding to earn them.) How little had he known when he'd blazed that first trace last summer that a road might save his son's life. Without relaxing his attention on his horses, he debated agonizingly the likelihood that Wood Fern could or would come to care for Simon Peter, concluding that the haughty Jacob would not let her.

He'd been to the No-Sah-We-Quet home twice the previous summer, but now the inadequacy of the one-room slab structure, nestled with similar homes of the Potawatomi on the snowy river-bank, struck him with dismay. Nearing the Indian settlement, he looked between the now plodding horses' ears at the cluster of huts and thought, I can't leave my baby here to freeze and starve. I'll turn around and go back to The Forks and see the other women.

But there was no place to turn the inexperienced team except on the frozen river, and the bank at that spot was steep. He drove on through a breaker of yapping dogs to the place where the No-Sah-We-Quet men were sitting in the sun in front of their shacks, constructing bark maple sap pails. The gray horses whinnied and received an answer from two emaciated Indian ponies digging through the snow for dry grass in a small clearing across the river.

Aaron pulled up his horses and stepped down from the sleigh to stand at their heads. "I can't leave these critters for a minute," he told the Indians, "they're only half broke and afraid of the dogs."

"I hear you lose two good horse in water, too bad," Jacob commented but with no particular feeling.

"Yes." Then pointing to the bucket in Jacob's hand, Aaron asked, "You'll go sugaring soon?"

Jacob flung his hand toward the iron kettle tipped against the shack. "Pile lumber, buy kettle, pony and auger. Make camp in maple trees soon."

"Jacob, I have to ask you something, is your wife well?"

"Sure, she got baby boy."

"I got baby boy too, but my wife is very sick."

"Potawatomi don't have so much baby like white people, feel good every time."

Aaron ignored the jab. "My baby doesn't have anything to eat."

"Your wife die?"

"We hope not, but her milk is dried up. Our cow gives no milk."

A knowing look crossed Jacob's face. "You want Wood Fern take your baby?" he asked and went into the pine slab shed when Aaron nodded.

Aaron waited, listening to the excited Potawatomi conversation inside.

Presently, Wood Fern came out with her baby wrapped in a wool blanket. She came within a few feet of Aaron and showed him a fat black-eyed child about two months old. "His name is John," she said.

"Could you come to the Landing and nurse our baby?" Aaron asked. "We have money."

"We talk," she pointed to Jacob. "You bring baby here, you bring flour and beans."

"Bring small stove and oil lamp," Jacob interrupted.

"Bring black woman's medicine," Fern went on. "You got chicken eggs and bacon? Bring. I feed your baby. I eat two times, one for your baby and one for mine."

"When does your cow give milk?" Jacob interposed.

"When the wild strawberries are ripe."

"That time we bring baby back to you," Fern said. "Bring berries too."

"You no see your baby till then," Jacob added emphatically.

"I promise." Aaron looked at the slender young woman, seeing the small, but full and round, brown breasts under the buckskin of her tunic. Simon Peter was twice as big as John, would he be slighted and starved? Then he remembered that many women nursed twins of necessity. He would bring Wood Fern tins of canned peaches and a bag of rolled oats in addition to the foods she'd asked for, praying the rest of the Potawatomi clan would not latch onto the windfall. He'd bring enough so there'd be no doubt.

"Bring dry moss," Fern said and went into her house.

"I brought some hay for your ponies," Aaron told Jacob. "Where do you want me to unload it?"

When the bales had been tossed off the sleigh, he turned the team around on the frozen river and drove through slashings between dark walls of timber to the sawmill town. The sun shone warmly on his face, and the horses lowered their eyelids against the glare. He whipped them up; he must hurry so Olaf could help him get Simon Peter back to the Indian camp before the sun dove behind the huge maples and hemlocks all along the road.

The return trip would accumulate about sixty miles of travel for the young horses in one long day. Aaron slapped their fat rumps with the reins and saluted their durable Percheron stock.

When he drove into the Landing after visiting the No-Sah-We-Quets, his father was standing in the barnyard. The older man's lips trembled with distress and his speech was distorted by heavy Scandinavian accents. "Dorcas says you gave Simon Peter to the Indians," he broke in before Aaron could speak. "I say, no, no. They will never bring him back."

"Pa, you know I had to do something. For God's sake, forget about the Indians and tell me how Liza is; I've been gone for seven hours." He was attempting to unhitch the barn-bent horses with the reins secured in one hand.

A softer look crossed his father's craggy face. "She doesn't cough so much, but she can't eat; she just lays there."

Olaf came around a corner of the cooperage, a light in his eyes for the first time since Mandy came down with typhoid. "Did you find a nursing mother for our boy?" he inquired hopefully. "Here, I'll help you get the horses into the barn."

"I found one; you'll have to help me get the baby to the No-Sah-We-Quets as soon as we can gather up some things and get started. Feed each horse half a pail of oats, no hay."

"You saw Wood Fern?"

"I did. She'll take care of the baby."

"Like her own?"

"She says she will. Where's Uncle Stephan and August? They have to dismantle the little heating stove in Stephan's cabin. Everybody's got to jump so we can leave here in an hour."

In the house, Aaron looked at the crumpled face of his fussing and hungry son and his nerve failed him completely; he could never take Simon Peter to the drafty shack of Wood Fern. But reason remonstrated; how could he or anyone else on the shore provide proper nourishment for the little boy? He picked the baby up and, swaying and crooning, held the warm body. Without food, the man-to-be he held against his breast would shrivel and grow cold. God, help us: he groaned in his soul. Then he remembered, a Loving Providence had foreseen their plight even before he and Liza had come together. God had given life to Jacob's seed in Wood Fern at exactly the right time. Now with the help of abundant food, Fern would be able to feed both babies.

A wave of shame came over him at his lack of faith; had he ever thought that because Fern was an aborigine, she was less than human? No, but somewhere in the back of his mind, the suspicion had lurked, demanding to be let in.

Dorcas was beckoning from the bedroom doorway. "Liza wants to see you again."

He laid the temporarily soothed baby in the cradle and went to his wife, kneeling by the bed and lifting her head. Garnet had cut Liza's long heavy hair and she'd lost so much weight, she looked and felt like a very sick child. "Aaron...Aaron," she managed to gasp, "you'll take...Simon Peter to...Wood Fern?"

"I will, Honey, Fern's going to keep our baby for a few weeks, like I told you."

"You'll take him today?"

"As soon as everyone can help Olaf and me get ready."

He kissed her and withdrew his arm from behind her head which fell back on the pillow. He smoothed back her damp, straggling hair and straightened up. "Olaf and I'll take good care of your baby and I'll see you sometime tonight."

Then he was inspired by an intelligence beyond himself. He went to the cradle in the kitchen, took the baby up again and carried him in and laid him on Liza's arm, placing the warm temple of their son within reach of her lips.

Her smile shook him with its angelic aspect. "Tell Wood Fern..." she said with her remaining strength and her arm fell limply beside the bundled baby.

Aaron checked the loaded sleigh and the trip line to the fractious off-horse's front leg. Garnet followed, plying him with instructions to be relayed to Wood Fern. Their father and Dorcas were fetching Simon Peter from the house. Without a word of warning, surprising Dorcas, Leander took the baby from her and walked past the sleigh to Helga's temporary grave. Dorcas started after him in alarm.

"Don't," Aaron cautioned her. "He'll be back in a minute."

The grandfather stood by the cairn of ice for a moment with his quiet bundle, then he returned to the sleigh. "I show Simon Peter to Mama," he explained calmly. "She'll be gone when he comes back to us in the spring."

Then fumbling, hindered by tears, he lifted the suddenly screaming infant to Olaf waiting on the seat of the sleigh. Aaron loosed the reins a fraction and the gray horses slammed into their collars.

23

I Knew You Could

At supper Leander spread blackberry preserves on one of Garnet's crusty biscuits. The jam recalled the day in August when Helga had made it from berries brought to the fishery by the No-Sah-We-Quets. It was only one more step in his memory train to Simon Peter, and articulating his thoughts aloud as he often did of late, he said to the eight others seated around the table, "Well, our baby is a month old today."

In answer, he heard Garnet mutter into her potato and whitefish chowder, "We'uns got no baby, Indians keep him."

"I guess you don't have to worry about Simon Peter," Olaf said evenly, without pausing in the business of eating.

Sitting at the end of the table with Liza, Aaron half rose from his chair and said caustically, "Well, Olaf, anytime now you can tell us why we don't have to worry about our baby."

"I was going to. When Gunnar brought that load of stave blanks this afternoon, he said a timber cruiser came into The Forks with a story about the new Potawatomi family up the river who was raising a bright little white baby with one of their own."

Leander saw Liza's head come up and two looks cross her face in succession, relief and longing. She'd never really seen the strapping son who'd been so much trouble to bring into the world. Aaron patted his wife's hand. "The wild strawberries'll be ripe before you know it. Take your time; it'll be two more months before you get back strength to lift that young man out of his cradle."

"If dat Indian squaw give him his share of de milk," Garnet put in pessimistically.

"She will," Aaron assured all who doubted. "And that news

137

makes up my mind," he went on with sudden enthusiasm; "the first thing tomorrow, I'm going to start to Marinette and see if the horse dealer we got Dick and Dan from still has that pair of Hackney ponies."

"What do we need with more horses to feed?" Olaf wanted to know.

"Pa," Aaron turned to his father, "You recollect those little bay horses?"

"Aye," Leander answered, "I said, if Mama was living, and now that we got a road, I'd buy them for her."

"Well, we're going to try to get them anyway," Aaron spoke eagerly. "If those geldings are still for sale, I'm going to get one for Liza and Naomi to use around here and one for Wood Fern."

Olaf objected to Aaron's plan immediately, "How're you going to keep Jacob from riding Fern's pony to death?"

That kept Aaron in thought for a moment, then he countered, "I'll tell him Hackneys are women's horses, which they are in certain parts of the east."

Leander felt he had to caution his optimistic son, "Those Indians'll starve a farm-raised horse."

"I thought of that," Aaron replied; "Jacob would have to agree to let us winter the pony with our stock."

"You couldn't give the pony to the Potawatomi till they brought Simon Peter home in good shape," Olaf said.

"That's where you're wrong," Aaron flung back. "If those ponies are gentle, as I believe they are, I want Fern to have one to bring the baby home with."

"Say, Pa," he proposed in the next breath, "why don't you get a good rest tonight and go along with me in the morning. It'll be our first trip out with the wagon this spring."

"I can't go away from here now."

"Pa, you can't do anything about Ma till May. A few days on the road would do you good."

Leander knew that. "I'll go," he replied. "You'll take Mama away from me when the time comes, anyway."

Leander sat on the seat of the lurching wagon, relieved that the foxy team was behaving for once. Frost-heaved, the stretch of cedar swamp corduroy was as rough as a lane of boulders between the lingering banks of snow. Once on the high land of the Bay de Noc Road, the trace became slick where the sun had melted the night frost. Leander sniffed tentatively after they'd rumbled southwest through the tall timber for half a mile. "I smell wood smoke."

Aaron too had inhaled the scent on the fresh April air. "I guess the Indians are back in the old sugaring camp; it's that time of year."

Around another bend in the road, high whinnies of welcome to the wagon team sounded through the tall bare-branched trees.

"Look, Pa!" Aaron cried in surprise. "Those are Jacob's little horses."

Leander's eyes followed Aaron's pointing finger and made out the ragged hides of two black and white spotted ponies tethered in the dry grass at the edge of receding snow in a forest glade.

The work team answered the ponies and Aaron slapped them into a jogging trot. "Now we've got a good excuse to talk to Jacob and ask him how Simon Peter's doing back on the Big Cedar." Relief and eagerness was in his voice.

Leander was not so hopeful. "Maybe he won't talk, even if we do see him."

"He'd better."

Then, a hundred paces to the right, they saw it through the ranked boles of maple trees, a tattered canvas stretched over bent and tied maple saplings and snuggled against a low gravel ridge. Smoke wafted from the peak opening of the tent and drifted in swirls to the ground. "That smoke means the Indians will get wet before tomorrow," Leander noted. "Maybe we'll get caught in the rain too."

"They don't have much of a shelter, do they?" Aaron observed.

"There's Wand-Dah-Sega, he boils sap with his woman," Leander raised his arm in the direction of the elderly couple stirring something in the precious iron kettle steaming on a rock hearth.

Every hard maple in sight had been equipped with a hollow sumac spile and a birchbark bucket. But a great spreading tree standing away from the direction of the smoke had two additional appendages hanging from a low horizontal limb.

"My God! they can't have those babies out here in this frosty weather!" Panic was rising in Aaron's voice.

"I don't think those are babies," Leander sought to reassure his son. But the bundles *were* babies, of course. He could see the little forms blanketed and thonged to the cradle boards.

"Pa, they've got Simon Peter swinging like a trussed turkey from that tree." Aaron groaned and pulled up the horses.

There was a sudden yapping on the south side of the road and they saw Jacob and Fern approaching with four large buckets of sap. Several mongrel dogs darted about with warning growls, snapping at the horses' heels. Jacob called the dogs off and set his buckets down on Aaron's side of the wagon. Fern walked on up the rise to the hollowed log collection vat.

"What do you want?" Jacob asked bluntly.

"We're on our way to town," Aaron answered in a level tone. "We didn't even know you were here."

But Leander knew Aaron was ready to dash to the tree and cut his son down.

"I say you no see baby till we bring him home." Jacob was indulging himself in a small retaliation for the harm other white men had done his people.

Leander felt the wagon seat move as Aaron braced his feet in frustration.

Jacob's sharp eyes too had taken in Aaron's emotional reaction to his hint of an ultimatum, and he continued deliberately, "But Fern say you have small look at baby. He sleep, you no wake."

In spite of the distraction of the Potawatomi's noisy travois ponies, Aaron tied the grays to a tree. "Don't rush up there like you're afraid the baby's being neglected," Leander warned him. "I'll stay by the horses in case those dogs come back."

"No, we'll go see Simon Peter together."

At that moment, Alec No-Sah-We-Quet and his wife Rose came out of the woods with their burdens of maple juice. Alec acknowledged the Johannsens' presence with a bare nod of the head. Leander held back so Aaron would keep a respectful distance as they followed the Indians to the sugaring fire.

"Hello, hello, friends," Wand-Dah-Sega greeted them and motioned for his wife to serve the guests each a steaming cup of the half-boiled-down sap.

Leander smacked his lips to show appreciation and signaled with his eyebrows for Aaron to do the same. "Good, good," he complimented the sugar makers, but his mind sent another message, what are you waiting for? Show us our son and grandson.

Rose and Mrs. No-Sah-We-Quet went into the shelter, but Fern stood aside and spoke to the little girls, Martha and Marie, who went to the dangling cradles and swung them lightly. But there was no sound; incredibly, in the near freezing air, the two babies were sleeping.

Pretending his son was not ten feet away, Aaron held his hot cup of sap in a toasting gesture to Jacob. "Sweet," he said. "It tastes good."

"Sap run good this year," Jacob said proudly. "Cold night, warm day makes good sugar." Then a calculating gleam came in his eye. "You buy sugar."

"Yes, as much as you can spare."

"We bring sugar when we bring baby and strawberries. You got dollar now?"

Leander found himself reaching in his pocket, but Aaron was already fishing a gold piece from the waistband of his trousers, explaining as he offered it, "Many dollar."

Jacob grinned. "I know, much dollar to buy new tent."

There was still no sound from the cradles. Leander could see that Aaron was reluctant to break his word by asking to see the baby. Well he, Leander, had made no promise. "We'll just peek at our baby and go away so you can get your work done," he told Jacob.

At that, Wood Fern beckoned them closer and lifted a blanket flap from one of the babies' faces. It was Simon Peter, plump-faced and sound asleep.

"And here is John." Fern went to the other cradle and showed them a small but fat and brown infant. "I don't have enough milk for two such big boys," she explained casually. "So I give them soup made of pounded dried venison and the oatmeal and peaches you bring. Baby grow good, yes?"

"Yes, Wood Fern, baby grow good," Aaron complimented sincerely.

"You tell your wife?"

With a nod, Aaron wheeled with tears in his eyes and said, "Well Pa, I guess we got to go see a man about a horse."

Leander willed Helga to see him as he carried two stave buckets of water from the bay to the barrel of cow droppings in the corner of her flower garden. The white terrier ran past the gill net garden fence to the rear of the woodshed where a piece of mainsail with a red stripe covered the sawdust and ice on the pine coffin. There the dog paused, dropping to his haunches with a low, knelling whine that sent liquid grief down Leander's spine and back up through his chest. "Tippy come away from there," he ordered, and the dog bounded up to be petted.

"It'll soon be over," he said to the dog. "We should've shut you up the day we carried Mama out here."

He looked up shore at the aspen greening against the darker cedars on the point. On the coming May Sunday, if the weather was fit for sailing, a flotilla of fishing boats would sail east from the Michigan shore to Ephraim where Helga's funeral would be held in the Moravian church with their old friends present. It had not been a year since she sailed west to the new fishery.

He walked around to enter the garden gate then looked up at the sound of his name being called. Naomi, her bonnet and pinafore flying, was running over the log bridge from the cooperage where she'd been reading her morning lesson to Olaf.

"Come, Tippy," she said to the dog when he trotted to her, "we'll help Grandpa Johannsen fix Grandma's flowers."

Leander was deeply aware of the worth of family as he swung around to greet her; family was what life was all about. Friends and kin, work and integrity, vision and abiding faith could make a man out of a bone-strung mass of flesh and rebuild a nation near mortally wounded by civil war. He'd come to America to find these things for his loved ones and now, five months after his feet had been swept from the deck, the dream was taking shape again. The sound of hammers on August Greutzmacher's cabin reminded him of that. It would be good to have Eva Strauss marry the stonemason and cooper and bring her nephew to join the Johannsen crew.

Naomi's sails were furled by the cessation of her forward movement. "I'll help you, Grandpa," she offered cheerfully. "I did it last year when I was much smaller."

He winced, remembering the day of his tantrum over the barrel, but he told her, "Well now, you take this piggin of fertilizer I've drawn from Grandma's green-barrel and water those heartsease over there. Do you remember what your grandma used to call those little purple fellows with the yellow faces?"

"I know!" Naomi shrilled excitedly. "She said they were Johnny-jump-ups."

"Aye, she did." He looked out to sea, past the location of Aaron and Bjorn in the pound boat, to the long strip of Wisconsin floating on the horizon. "We're going to dig the heartsease and the little blue flags and plant a flower blanket for grandma in Ephraim."

"Ma says Grandma's box'll be in the ground there." A small frown flitted over Naomi's brown face.

"Aye, 'tis so. But tell me. Where will your grandma really be besides beyond that star you watch with Garnet at night?"

"Garnet told me; Mandy, Grandma and my first daddy live in my heart."

"That, they do."

The child looked up at him speculatively, a question in her dark eyes, "Do you think those Indians put that little boy baby we had last winter in the ground?"

He bent to a child for the first time since Bjorn was a toddler. "No, little girl. What gave you that idea? We took Simon Peter to Wood Fern so she would feed him while your mama was so sick."

"And our cow didn't have no milk, neither?"

"That's the way it was."

He bent to the spigot on the barrel to draw his own bucket of "tea", as Helga had called the solution, and poured it in a shallow trench surrounding the reddish shoots of the white peony Helga had cherished above her other flowers. It was then that he heard his wife laugh.

Daily now in the warm days of June, Liza and Naomi, mounted double, rode the Hackney pony bareback along the beach or back to the old Indian sugar camp to pick trilliums. The little bay horse was so reliable that Naomi sometimes rode easily on the twin pillows of his rump. Dundee never lifted a foot or laid back an ear in anger, but he was lonesome for his lifetime partner, Jock. From the first, Leander had been uneasy about the treatment Jock would get from the No-Sah-We-Quets. Olaf said Indians simply did not understand how to treat animals.

Today as he worked at the ceaseless mending of nets on the beach, Leander watched Liza and Naomi ride toward him from down the shore. Liza pulled the little horse up beside the long net strung between two posts and spoke happily, "Isn't this a beautiful day after the rain?" She had almost recovered from her ordeal in March.

"It is. Did you girls have a nice ride?"

"Oh, yes, we got brave enough to swim Dundee across that crick and ride on to the place where you and Olaf came ashore in the fog."

Naomi took her arms from her mother's waist and slid back

to the pony's tail. "Simon Peter'll be big enough to ride Dundee by the time he gets home," she said.

Suddenly, Dundee tensed alarmingly, threw up his head and squealed like a stallion. Liza slid off his back and reached for Naomi. The pony flared his nostrils, snorting and scenting the air, and pawed the ground before he whinnied piercingly again. He'd heard or smelled something. Was it a bear or some strange manifestation of weather? Leander wondered. Then there were answering equine calls from out past the hemlocks on the corduroy road.

Before Liza could get the reins over Dundee's head, he was gone, head up, black mane and tail flying in the wind, crossing the mouth of the brook with tremendous splashes. Leander pocketed his cedar needle and hurried with Liza and Naomi up to the coopershop where they told Olaf what had happened, and on across the log bridge to the wagon road. Before they could set out to apprehend the little horse, he came galloping back, coaxing like a dog for them to come and see what he'd found.

I'll catch him for you," Leander shouted to Liza, but the compact bay horse snorted, evaded all hands and darted back on the trail.

"I'll stay here and watch if he comes back," Olaf offered, joining them.

"Naomi, you go on the porch of our house and stay there," Liza instructed her daughter. "Keep Tippy with you. I might get hold of Dundee in the woods."

Leander trotted along the wagon tracks through the hemlocks, almost reaching the low-bridged ash swale when the commotion erupted. Before he could step completely out of the way, Dundee came charging home with a yapping, shrieking, yelling stampede behind him. He'd found his partner Jock and was leading him to the shed they'd shared for a month in the spring. Wood Fern hung desperately but futilely to Jock's lead rope. The two No-Sah-We-Quet ponies, dragging Alec and Jacob, followed single-mindedly.

Wheeling at Liza's scream behind him, Leander saw with horror the nature of the cargo on the tail end of Jock's pole-and-thong travois. Packed in between bundles of camp gear and baskets of maple sugar, there were two babies laced to cradle boards. Simon Peter and little John were wailing in terror.

Trailing Jock, the spotted ponies, sleek and sassy from June grass and laden with similar burdens, shook off their handlers in the melee. Fern had lost her grip on Jock.

Bounding after the horses, Leander saw Olaf allow Dundee to pass at the edge of the clearing so he could snatch for Jock's bridle. This move only deflected the Hackney to the right and into the potato patch behind the two cabins on the north side of the brook. The other horses pounded ahead in a straight line in front of the houses toward the log-railed span over the fifteen-foot-wide stream.

The little No-Sah-We-Quet girls had fallen off their travois, but Rose's toddler Timmy was still clinging to the swerving travois of one spotted pony.

The barking Indian dogs flashed ahead of the horses and jumped Tippy from behind. Heedless of being ripped to pieces, Naomi rushed to his defense. Leander sprinted as he had not in forty years. Well ahead of the Potawatomi, he kicked the dogs from Tippy and shoved Naomi back to the stoop and dashed on.

Liza, with Wood Fern behind her, had gone leaping around the house after Jock as he tore down the barely greening early potato rows and into the lettuce, peas and onions. Racing toward the bridge to intercept the Hackney dragging the two babies, Leander glimpsed the frantic women through the space between the cabins. Liza and Fern were stumbling and grasping, trying to free their infants from the bounding travois.

Alec had shot ahead fast enough to catch the pony hauling his son Timmy and had eared that animal to a standstill.

Dundee pounded across the bridge with the Indian pony that had dumped the two little girls. The pony's travois hit the butt end of the bridge railing-log, throwing maple sugar and wild strawberries onto the dock and into the water. By that time, Dan, the wilder of the two Johannsen work horses, had sailed over his pole fence and was kicking at the Potawatomi pony by the cooperage.

Meanwhile, Wood Fern's Hackney Jock was plunging past Helga's flower garden, searching for an avenue to the bridge. Veering between the woodshed and the garden, a shaft tip caught in the fence netting. He tore loose from that entrapment and was imminently about to make the same mis-maneuver with his precious load of freight that the spotted pony had made.

A prayer burst from Leander, "God, help us!" This petition was answered instantly by a supernatural burst of speed and strength and his creaky body was airborne. Once he had contact

146

with Jock's bridle, he held on, his sagging weight dragging the horse's head down.

From a haze of dizzy determination, he finally heard Stephan say, "Let go, Leander, let go. I'll hold the horse."

Dimly he knew Jacob, Liza and Fern were cutting the sobbing babies loose from the tangled netting and binding thongs. The Hackney was quiet now. Leander left the horse to Stephan and found an overturned fish box on the dock. He sat down, his legs quivering, his heart pounding painfully, trying to get his mind together, but everyone was talking to him at once.

"Pa," Olaf said with feeling choking his voice, "You saved Aaron's little boy."

Liza was laying the buckskin clothed baby in his lap. "Here, Papa Johannsen, here's your grandbaby."

Garnet had run back for his cap and was setting it askew on his roan head to protect it from the hot June sun. "You done run like a young man," she said admiringly.

Then someone called to him from over the water. At first he thought it was Aaron sailing in with a load of fish. But it was Helga. "I knew you could," she said in tender praise.